K.M. Jackson

FROM HERE TO SERENITY

Published by Shakey Red's Rock
Originally Published by Dafina in *Holiday Temptation*, 2016
Re-print 2021
ISBN: 978-1-956721-07-2

Interior Design by JW Manus
www.kmjackson.com

Other titles by K.M. Jackson

The Creative Hearts Series

Book 1: *Through The Lens*

Book 2: *Seduction's Canvas*

Book 3: *Threads of Desire*

Loving On The Edge Series

Bounce

Bounce Back

The Unconventional Brides Series

Insert Groom Here

To Me I Wed

The Betting Vow

How To Marry Keanu Reeves in 90 Days

Real Men Knit

Chapter 1

"A panic attack? You have got to be joking. Ross Montgomery doesn't panic." Ross ended his third-person statement by giving the young, pale-faced intern doing a spot-on Doogie Howser impersonation a withering look.

"I, well, I'm sorry, Mr. Montgomery. But it's what our data says," Doogie stammered out.

Ross turned to the nurse fiddling by his bedside, poking at him in a most uncomfortable way. She was brown-skinned and petite, with generous curves and alert brown eyes that seemed to miss nothing. Her bleached-blond, highly teased and sprayed bob was in sharp contrast to her deep skin tone. "Can't you get me someone else, honey?" Ross asked, adding extra molasses to his deep bass. "The kid here obviously doesn't know what he's talking about. As a matter of fact, I'm waiting for my private doctor, Dr. Nair, to come in. Can you go and check on her?" Ross gave the nurse a quick wink and his killer smile. It was the same one that usually had women either melting or jumping to do his bidding. But his smile stopped midstream when he caught blondie's brow raise and her sharp eyes go dead cold.

"Save it, handsome. Neither you nor doc over here is giving out any orders. I'm on a schedule," she said, sending a nod the young doctor's way and getting tight lips by way of a retort. "Now hold still while I get your temp and take your pressure."

Ross suppressed a retort, thinking it wise to clam up and let the woman do what she had to do and move on. Besides, he could respect schedules and taking care of business.

He opened his mouth for her to stick the thermometer under his tongue and dutifully gave over his arm. He knew when he was beat. He also knew going any further with the no-nonsense nurse would be a waste of energy. And he hated wasting energy. One of the things he prided himself on was being efficient. Efficient and a moneymaker. And right now, while lying in a hospital bed, being told that he indeed was *not* having what he could have sworn was a heart attack, when he was this close to closing a billion-dollar deal, he was being anything but efficient. Ross's jaw tightened at the thought.

"Hey there, Thor, you want to loosen up a bit so that I can get the thermometer back out." The nurse—Ross looked at her nametag now—Nurse Edwards was directing this at him.

"I don't see why I need this," Ross replied by way of mouth opening. "If it's just a panic attack, you might as well let me go now and stop wasting all our time."

Dr. Doogie and Nurse Edwards shared glances, and then Doogie finally spoke up. "Yes, according to our preliminaries, it was not a heart attack but a panic-induced episode triggered, most likely, by stress and other contributors. If we could just go over your diet for the week? With some changes, there are ways to nip this in the bud before it becomes a bigger problem."

Changes? Ross inwardly bristled at the word. His life was perfect as it was. He was a successful businessman, well on his way to making the *Forbes* magazine list within the next few years. Who knew, not long after that, maybe even surpassing his father's accomplishments, if not ever getting his esteem? He was rich, free, and single. There was nothing in his life that needed changing.

Except Serenity.

Ross frowned as thoughts of his four-year-old daughter came to his mind once again. He was thinking of her when the pain gripped at his chest as he was on the phone with his investors. And it was her he was thinking of when he was being hooked up to electrodes and beeping machines.

When was the last time he'd seen her? It must be going on eight months now. Which was a huge hunk of a lifetime for a four-year-old, and with his current schedule he didn't see a visit anytime on the horizon. Sure, he sent her extravagant gifts for her birthday, but he'd heard it in her voice during his last call that she was unimpressed. The gifts could have been from anyone. All she could do during their last conversation was go on about how much fun she'd had with her mom, Yasmine, and her new dad, Devon, during their recent trip to Disneyland.

Hell, what did his daughter need with expensive gifts when Devon could give her the magic of Disneyland? Ross's hands balled into fists.

"Okay, Thor, there you go again. Your pressure is going sky high. That's not gonna get you out of here any quicker, you know?"

Ross gave Nurse Quick Mouth a hard look, which she countered back with one of her own. He was actually starting to admire her. Maybe he could find a place for her in his corporation. Lord knew she could freeze balls with that look.

"She's right, Ross, you need to relax," his friend and primary doc, Misha Nair, came in saying as she pushed the blue privacy curtain aside.

"I don't need anything, but for you to tell Doogie over here to sign my discharge papers so that I can get out of here."

Doogie gave a cough and Misha pursed her darkly stained lips together, causing Ross to note her carefully applied make-up. He also took notice of the fact that she wore what looked like a black cocktail dress under her open lab coat and high stiletto heels. Though always polished, this was not the jeans-and-sweats Misha he'd been buddies with since college. She took his chart from Doogie and quickly gave it a flip through.

"Did I interrupt a date?" he asked.

Misha ignored him and continued reading his chart before finally meeting his gaze. "What do you think, Ross? I'm not having the hell pinched out of my toes for the fun of it. I should have ignored your messages, but that bulldog of an assistant you have never gives up. I was afraid he'd track me at the restaurant if I didn't come over. Not that you weren't in fine hands with Dr. Stein here."

"How would I know that? This guy says I had a panic attack, which I know is not true. I never panic."

Misha rolled her eyes as Nurse "No Chill," still not amused, shook her head and removed the pressure cuff, making her exit with a wry chuckle.

"Ross, the numbers don't lie." Misha held up his chart. "These, along with your last physical reports from my office, are telling me it's time to make some real changes, or the next time you won't be so lucky, and it won't be a panic attack."

Ross sat up straighter, while at the same time he tried dismissing Misha's words. "Stop being so dramatic."

Misha moved closer and put her finger to his wrist to take his pulse. "*Dramatic* is having me pulled out of a dinner date, not that it was going anywhere. Freaking Internet can suck it. But smart is listening to your body and coming in to get checked out when you think something is wrong. Even smarter will be taking my advice. It's time for you to make changes." She looked him in the eye. "What exactly were you doing when this happened?"

"Nothing," Ross said as innocently as he could muster, which wasn't that innocent at all. "I was in the middle of a business call, negotiating the terms of a deal."

"And?"

"And what?"

Misha dropped his wrist and shook her head. "And you mean for me to believe that you weren't getting your pressure up as you were nailing some poor sap to a wall. What's the rest?"

Ross couldn't help his grin. She did know him well. "And I may have been having a bite while I was leaving the gym after a workout. You know how working out and making deals gives me an appetite."

For that, he got a punch in the arm, and Doogie gave Misha a look this time. "Dr. Nair?"

"It's okay, Stein. Mr. Montgomery and I go way back. I'll handle him."

Doogie shook his head, clearly annoyed at this dismissal. "Fine. He can go. Since you're his primary, I'll sign him over to you for the follow-ups with a consult to Dr. West in cardio." He made a few notes in the chart and handed it off to Misha before leaving.

Ross grinned and started to get up, but was stilled by Misha's firm hand on his chest.

"Not so fast. I didn't discharge you yet, Ross."

"Come on, Mish. What are you playing at? I can still get in some calls out to the Far East if I go now."

"This is serious, or at least it could have been. It's time to make a change. What did you have for lunch today?"

He frowned. "A pastrami from Sal's."

"And the day before?"

Ross gave her a look. She already knew it was the same, or a version of it. She knew his poor eating habits, but he balanced it out with tough physical workouts in the gym and twice-weekly boxing.

Seeming to know what he was thinking, Misha spoke. "Before you say it, sorry your workouts are not good enough to make up for the crap you put in your body. You're getting to the age where a workout can't make up for high-fat foods and chips. We're both not teens anymore."

"Fine, Mish, I'll clean up my act. You'll see."

"Bullshit those you can, Ross. Not me. And on top of it, you need to relax. You need a diet and a lifestyle cleanup. That's food and meditation. Less work, less stress, better food, and less caffeine."

Ross balked. "The devil you say, woman?"

Misha grinned. "Stop being such a big baby. It's the holidays coming up. Now's the perfect time. I want you to take a few weeks off and give the business a break."

Now it was Ross's turn to laugh. "Sorry. I've got a deal and clients I'm meeting over the holiday. I'm taking my new boat out to wine and dine them. You want to come?"

Misha glared. "Are you not hearing me? It's time to change. Your numbers are a mess. Your arteries are clogging as we speak. This is urgent, Ross."

"I hear you. But I have to make this deal happen. I can't let it go."

Misha shook her head, then looked at Ross dead-on. "What about Serenity?"

"That's not fair," Ross gritted out.

"I learned how to play from the best."

If it were anyone but his old friend, Ross would tell her off, or at least walk the hell out of there. But he couldn't with Misha.

"I'll tell you what," she said, reaching over to pull a small take-out box from her large tote, "though you interrupted my date, I did manage to snag dessert to go." She popped the top on a good-looking chocolate confection with cream on top and picked it up, holding it to Ross's lips. "Here, take a bite."

"What are you up to? First you want me to clean up my act and then you're trying to fatten me up with dessert?"

"Just shut up and listen for once. It's made by a friend of mine. She's a personal chef I met a few years back while on a yoga retreat. She specializes in low-fat, good-for-you food, and has really made a difference for quite a few of my patients."

Ross frowned at the mention of "low fat," and prepared himself for a mouthful of sawdust. But to quiet Misha, he leaned in and took a bite.

It was heaven. Soft and creamy, while rich and decadent. The flavors were sweet and sophisticated, calling him to reach for more.

Ross looked up at Misha. "What did you say this chef's name was?"

Misha grinned. "I didn't, but it's Essie Bradford. Her food is amazing and you'll never meet a sweeter, kinder, more Zen person. Let me call her. If she's free, I know she'll say yes. Essie just can't say no to a friend, and she is a friend, so don't mess it up," she warned.

He reached out and took the rest of the sweet from Misha's hand and snagged another delectable bite. "If she's half as sweet as this dessert, I'm sure we'll get along just fine."

Chapter 2

"You have got to be freaking kidding me. She sent back my soufflés? As if she would know a whip from a flake. I should go over there and tell her where she can shove—" Essie stopped short there, closed her eyes and did a few quick, deep cleansing breaths before she opened them again to see Trevor, one of the waiters, waiting with an apology in his kind eyes. Normally, he was all party-on and a quick gossip, but it would seem the nightmare from table twenty-three had taken the wind out of his sails, too. Essie not only wanted to give her a good tell-off for herself, but for Trevor as well. Besides, after getting home last night and practically tripping over her boyfriend's packed bags, she was in the mood to lash out.

Trevor raised a hand. "No, hon. I don't think you going over there will do any good. You know, as well as I, that the dessert is perfect. She's been complaining all night." Trevor slipped a look to the woman at twenty-three, who stared back at Essie in the open-air kitchen with a smug now-get-it-right look.

Seriously, some folks should not be allowed out in polite company without proper supervision.

Who sent back perfectly good chocolate soufflés? Not to mention the complaint she had about Essie's coq au vin, which had won awards. Heat rose in Essie's cheeks, and it had nothing to do with the fact it was sweltering in the prep line of her friend Julian's popular Westside bistro's kitchen. She knew she had to tamp down on her emotions. One, because it went totally against the Zen, no judgment, live-in-the-moment lifestyle she prided herself on. And two, because the kitchen was open and a focal point, on display to all the diners. This was normally a feature Essie enjoyed, but tonight, being as tired and emotionally raw as she was, she'd rather be anywhere but here on display for the New York IT crowd.

Essie had long told herself that if—*no, when*—she'd saved up enough money, coupled with the financial backing she needed to open her own place, she'd have a similar design. She was brought up to believe that the food prep was all a part of the dining experience and should be shared. Now, considering the nightmare at table twenty-three, who did nothing but complain about anything and everything, maybe that interaction would have to be rethought.

Once again, Essie let out a calming breath. She really shouldn't get mad at the terror on twenty-three. Though Essie knew the soufflé was perfect, she grabbed a clean spoon to take a taste to be sure before throwing the rest away, with regret over the wasted food. Yes, the soufflé was fine. Actually, better than fine, but it lacked a bit of her usual spark, and she blamed herself for that. She should have told Julian no, that she couldn't fill in when he called, begging for her to cover for his usual head chef, who had an emergency. That's what she got for always saying yes.

Essie was exhausted and she knew it, having just come back home to New York from two months on the road as the private chef to an up-and-coming rock band. Six members, all with different tastes: one vegan, one veg, the rest true carnivores. It was quite the demanding gig. And no sooner was she back in her apartment, dropping her well-worn duffel on the floor, only to have them collide with the bags and boxes belonging to her ex-boyfriend, Cameron. She guessed if she hadn't gotten in a few hours early, she may have found out about his planned relationship departure via text, which was his usual passive-aggressive modus operandi.

No, she wasn't mad at the complainer over at twenty-three. She was mad at herself for being so gullible and not seeing Cameron for what he was, a cheater with a penchant for large-chested, petite women and continuing far too long in a relationship she knew was ultimately going nowhere. She should have known something was up when he was the one to encourage her to say yes and take the job on the road with the band. Telling her how great the money would be, and how he'd come out to meet her on the road, which he never did. *Damn that Cam. Always the user.* They had met while in culinary school when he asked her to tutor him with sauce reductions.

The thought pulled Essie up short. He was another "yes" that she should have said "no" to. *Him, and the hims before.* Always ready to use her up until a better option came along. So many yeses that started with hope, but then led to disappointment.

Just as she should have said no to Julian, and it would have spared her tonight's aggravation. Not to mention she could have been catching up on much-needed sleep. Yep, each time she put her own needs aside and gave in to the "yes" to satisfy others, it didn't turn out well. She was over being everyone's go-to "yes."

It was time she started living for herself.

Essie let out a breath before stepping forward, reaching for another just baked soufflé and topping it with powdered sugar, extra berries, and a drizzle of chocolate. She looked up and carefully handed it to Trevor with a weary smile. "Let's hope this time's the charm."

Trevor let out a sigh. "I doubt she'd know charm if it landed in her lap."

As she watched him walk over to table twenty-three, the woman made brief eye contact with Essie. Her clear blue eyes met Essie's own dark brown ones before she gave Essie a nod of triumph and took a bite. The woman smiled, a small, satisfied, smug grin, which made the hairs on the back of Essie's neck stand up a bit, and had her biting the inside of her lip. But Essie let it go as Trevor turned back her way and gave her his wide grin and a little thumbs-up.

People. Some just have to believe they're that extra-special snowflake or they'll melt away to nothing. She shrugged, trying to let the encounter roll off her back. Who knew? Maybe Ms. Twenty-three had a bad day, or a bad month, or her boyfriend of two years did a dump-and-dash. Shit happened.

Julian came and leaned over the counter, his piercing green eyes sparkling with both weariness at the late hour and excitement over the packed restaurant. "Essie, my love, thank you so much for filling in tonight and tomorrow. I know it's been a madhouse, but you saved my hide, like you will never know. I owe you big-time."

"Yes, you do. I'll add it to your list." She smiled, now feeling bad for thinking so harshly of him. He'd always been a good friend, and the money from tonight would be a help, now that she didn't have Cam's money coming in to share the rent. Not that he wasn't late, most of the time, anyway.

The thought of Cam and money made her wonder if her dream of having her own place would ever come true. Back when she was with him, they talked about opening up a place together. She couldn't help but wonder how she could do it alone now.

Essie fought to push the thought aside. It was almost too much to deal with, just one day back and one day into the breakup. As of now, she'd operate as she had. At least he picked a good time. She was solvent and would not need to work until after the holidays, when she had more private jobs lined up. For now she'd do what she so very much needed to do for herself: a blissful holiday to think things over and sort out her life. One where she would not have to serve others, but, instead, visit with her mother and enjoy being the one who was fed, nourished, and treated right for a change.

So when her phone rang as she was ending the night with Julian, and it was her friend Misha with a call about a job cooking for some rich bigwig over the Christmas vacation, Essie was only too happy to put her first "no" into practice.

Chapter 3

Maybe it was the momentary hush that came over the restaurant, or maybe it was something else, but for some reason Essie looked up from where she was putting a final touch of sauce on a simple roasted chicken before it was to go out, and saw the hostess, Nikki, escorting a striking couple to table twenty-three.

Her unlucky table.

As she watched the gorgeous couple take their seats, Essie couldn't help but notice how compatible they seemed, in contrast to how she and Cam must have looked together. The woman was tall and statuesque, more legs than anything else, with glistening golden-brown skin and a figure that was shown off well by the few artfully draped pieces of fabric that adorned her body, despite the biting winter chill outside. Essie's gaze wavered to the tall, dark figure in the expensively cut business suit. She involuntarily sucked in a breath, caught in her not-so-hidden perusal, as the male counterpart of this couple was, for some reason, looking directly at her, too.

His deep-set, dark eyes locked on Essie's, and across the expanse of the dining room and over the heads of the other diners, Essie could have sworn she felt something in that moment that was strangely like a touch. She reached up and ran her hand across the side of her neck as he gave her the slightest of nods. One side of his beautiful mouth quirked up in the most devilish way to let her know that yes, he was looking at her, and yes, she should take note of it. Essie's cheeks flushed hot, as if something dangerously like desire mixed with a twinge of anger flicked at her center.

What is up with that smile? Sit with your model, Mr. Rich, and leave the smiles for your date.

Essie nibbled at her bottom lip and turned away from the scene, quickly inspecting the chicken that was just put up for an order, then turning her attention to the sauce for her Bourguignon. One stipulation she didn't budge on when agreeing to help Julian out was the fact that she ran the kitchen her way. So for the nights she was filling in, Essie made sure to double check each dish after it was plated, be it savory or dessert. No matter the name on the restaurant's exterior, the food was still a representation of her reputation.

"Oh, my God, do you know who that is?" Trevor said as he came over to the window, practically bouncing out of his shoes.

She knew he was talking about the couple at table twenty-three, but Essie tried to appear cool and unconcerned. She had a reputation and beef to concentrate on. And not the kind Trevor was pushing, mind you.

"No, should I?" Essie let her gaze smoothly slide around Trevor, not at the man, but at the beautiful woman by his side. Now that she thought about it, she was sure she'd seen her on the cover of some magazine or another. And judging by the way some of the other patrons were gawking, she was probably right. The young woman may be famous, but she was clearly into the man. Leaning in, she was rubbing the back of his neck with one hand, while the other disappeared under the table, only to come up abruptly when he seemed to be, well, Essie could only guess by the girl's pretty pout, unmoved. She looked away from the couple back to Trevor. "She is pretty."

Trevor waved an impatient hand. "Oh, she's all right, but it's him I'm talking about. That's Ross Montgomery, the man of the millennium." Essie frowned. He was good-looking, but, come on, millennium? She didn't have time for this.

But Trevor continued. "And baby boy is paid with a capital *P.* He's been taking over real estate all up and down the East Coast, and with his taste in the latest beauty de jour, he's become a fixture on the gossip scene, too."

Essie was busy on her next dish when what Trevor said really hit her, and she suddenly stopped mid-glaze. *Wait. Ross Montgomery.* Wasn't the client Misha called her about last night named Ross Mont-something or other? She took another peek at table twenty-three, only to catch Mr. Millennium once again staring back at her.

"Holy hell," Essie hissed.

"That's what I'm saying," Trevor said, his voice now taking on a conspiratorial tone. "And he seems pretty interested in you. Asked that you be pointed out special."

"Crap." Oh, God. Mr. Tall, Dark, and Rich as All Get-Out was here, and he was checking her out. But as unexpected butterflies fluttered in her belly, Essie frowned. What was he doing here, checking her out? And checking her out at the tail end of a long dinner shift when she looked like who knew what? Not that it should matter. She'd turned Misha down last night, and she'd meant it. Her no meant *no.* It was high time her friends got to know the new, improved, more assertive Essie.

She would enjoy these few holiday weeks off, and then it was back to the grind with clients in January. She'd worked hard enough and would enjoy this well-deserved holiday. It didn't matter how rich—she peeked at table twenty-three again—or how good-looking the client was. She turned back to Trevor. "So, did Mr. Millennium even order anything?"

Trevor's eyes went wide. "Did he ever? Well, not that this has anything to do with you, but, of course, he ordered our most expensive champagne. But getting to your line of work, he and his"—Trevor paused dramatically—"date will be having caviar to start with, the foie gras, and the oyster tartar. From there, they will go on to the risotto and the sirloin. Then they are having the salmon and the cracked lobster."

Essie's jaw dropped. "Are you serious? There is no way two people are eating all of that."

"That's what I said," Trevor replied. "But the man wants what the man wants, so that's what you're making."

Essie let out a slow breath, long and slow through her nostrils, working to bring her equilibrium back, as she mentally went over the menu choices for table twenty-three. *I know what this is, mister,* she thought as her eyes once again slid over to where Mr. Montgomery was being touched and diddled by his young lady companion. She watched as Teagan, the sommelier, uncorked champagne to the model's delight and Mr. Montgomery's look of indifference.

Essie shook her head and smiled, now more confident that she'd made the right decision turning down the job from Misha last night. He seemed like a total spoiled jerk. And it didn't matter that he'd turned up here tonight in Julian's restaurant to test her food firsthand, and possibly offer her the job once again. Her no was firm. She took the order to get it going with the rest of the crew. She'd wasted enough time and, at least for tonight, he and everyone else were paying customers. As such, they'd get her very best.

❄ ❄ ❄

The meal was delicious, which was as Ross expected. The meat was tender, the fish was succulent, and everything was seasoned to perfection, leaving the most delicious lingering aftertaste in Ross's mouth. He already craved his next meal. Misha was right. He needed this chef in his life. Sneaky of Mish not to tell him what a pretty little thing the chef was. Pretty enough that, despite the fact his date for tonight was, Ross inwardly groaned now at the thought, this year's "Internet's Most Googled Body Under Thirty," his eyes kept wandering to the intriguing chef with the sweet smile.

There was something about her: smooth, rich umber toned skin, wispy bangs peeking out from under her bandana, which framed deep-set brown eyes, which somehow sparkled like diamonds in the dimly lit restaurant. She had a sharp, determined-looking nose, which led to luscious, full lips. When these opened into a wide smile, her lips seemed to take over her face and her smile brightened the entire restaurant with perfectly imperfect teeth that showed just a hint of the most endearing gap.

The owner, Julian, he remembered, now came by their table. “I hope you all enjoyed your meal. Can I interest you in anything else?”

Ross’s “yes” came out at the same time as his date’s “no,” leaving the owner smiling with awkward confusion. Ross righted the situation. “Yes, we would like dessert. What specials is the chef offering tonight?”

“I don’t want to stay for dessert,” Lela whined. “I thought we were heading down to the Bowery for the sneaker launch party. Everybody is going to be there and DJ Extasy is spinning tonight. I don’t want to miss that.” Lela gave her hair a twist around her finger and let her hand trail toward her breast.

Normally, the blatant come-on would be just the thing to rev Ross’s engines, but after last night, Ross was dog tired. All he really wanted to do was taste that pretty chef’s dessert and then get the hell home to sleep, so he could get into the office early tomorrow. The last thing he wanted to do was go to some silly sneaker launch party and hear a DJ with a misspelled name.

Ross let out a sigh. This was his fault. He shouldn’t have invited Lela out tonight and should have just come alone. Even if it was counter to his playboy image. That shit was getting tired anyway.

He reached into his pocket and peeled off a few hundred-dollar bills, then turned to his date and licked his lips before staring into her almond-shaped eyes. “I tell you what. You take my car and head over to the launch party and have a great time. Sorry, babe, but I’m not going to make it tonight.”

He watched as Lela pulled her lips together in a pretty little pout.

"Come on, Ross. I thought we'd make a night of this. Have a little fun. See and be seen, and then end it back at your place."

She trailed her hand up his knee and higher along his thigh. When she got close to the point of no return, he stilled her eager fingers with his own.

"Like I said, it's not happening tonight, sweetheart." Ross gently put the money in her hands. His eyes stopped any further comment.

Lela shrugged, seeming to know the conversation was now over, as was the evening. "Okay, I guess I won't be seeing you in the morning then." She made a point to hide any disappointment from her face. Her eyes shined bright as she smiled wide and leaned over to kiss his cheek before gracefully exiting from their prime table, sashaying out of the restaurant with her trademark supermodel walk.

Ross looked back to the owner. "Thank you. Everything was delicious. I'd like an assortment of the desserts, and please ask the chef, Essie, if she would kindly take a moment to join me."

❄ ❄ ❄

Join him!

Essie fumed more steam than the stainless-steel, industrial-grade pots surrounding her. Not that she didn't expect the special request, but still it rankled her nerves. Especially after seeing the way his date seemed to be dismissed. Still, Essie finished all the other orders and found herself taking special care with his. Why? It wasn't as if she had anything to prove.

As she followed behind Julian, who carried the desserts over, Essie fought not to pull down her smock or brush her hair behind her ear. Instead, she pushed her shoulders back, pulling herself up to her full five-seven height.

"Mr. Montgomery, here are your desserts, and may I introduce our chef for the evening, Essie Bradford," Julian said.

Essie was about to lean in and give him a quick handshake, when he surprised her by standing. His impressive height and broad shoulders made her feel fairly small as he reached out and took her hand gently in his own.

"It is my pleasure to make your acquaintance, Ms. Bradford."

His grip was warm and engulfing, his eyes dark and unnervingly unwavering, as he looked at her way too deeply for a person who wanted to talk about only her food. Essie fought to keep her chin up and not look down. She would not break contact. First to blink loses. And she knew losing to this man would not be good.

So she looked at him just as deeply, until something in him shifted and he let go of her hand, leaving her with a surprising chill. He stepped back to open space for her in the banquette. "Would you please sit with me for a moment? Join me for dessert?"

Essie looked at him with narrowed eyes as she walked around and purposefully went into the other end of the banquette and sat. "Sure, since you pretty much ordered everything on the menu."

He sat and Julian put down the desserts along with Trevor, who poured them each a glass of champagne before exiting.

"Well, after tasting the small bit from Misha last night, I had to have more. And seeing that you turned down my offer of employment flat, this seemed like the only way I'd get to sample all you had to offer."

Essie fought to ignore the instant rush of heat flaring through her body, and gave him a smile. "All? That's not nearly all." At his raised brow, the butterflies went swirling in Essie's belly again, and she shifted to tamp down on them. "And I'm sorry about turning down your offer, Mr. Montgomery, but I've been on the road for the past two months, and I really don't want to get on the road again. Especially not right now during the holidays."

"Please call me Ross. It's not like I'm your boss or anything. And I can totally respect you wanting to take a little time off after being on the road. But please understand, Ms. Bradford, I really do need your services. I don't know if Misha explained to you, but she called you from the ER. It's imperative that I get my diet and, as she tells it, my lifestyle in order, too. But I'm a busy man, and I can't afford to take the holidays off. This is a working one for me, like so many others, and I need to have a chef with me on this trip I'm taking."

Essie shook her head, partially to tell him no and partially to remind herself to stay strong in her new "NO" mode. "I really am so sorry, Mr. . . ." Essie paused, then said, "Ross. But I don't think I can do it. On the other hand, I can recommend to you some other quite capable chefs."

Ross reached over with his spoon and dipped into Essie's chocolate tart, taking a bite.

He closed his eyes, letting the flavor she knew so well permeate his senses. He smiled as he swallowed, looking like he was enjoying every moment before he opened his eyes and looked back. He reached for another spoon, this time bringing some of her mousse toward her lips. Essie's eyes went wide. "What are you doing?"

"You need to taste this."

Essie gave him a stern frown. "It's from tonight's specials and my own recipe so I have tasted it." For a moment she thought she saw something like a spark in his eyes.

"Yes, but when was the last time you *really* tasted it?"

Essie gave him a challenging stare to match his own. "Fine." She opened her mouth slightly, and before she could reach for the spoon, it was already to her lips. Rich and creamy. That's what it was, rich and creamy, with a hint of smokiness that exploded on her tongue in a perfect melody of notes. Essie closed her eyes and let the flavors hit her. *Damn, you did good, Essie,* she thought as it slid down her throat. *Real good.*

Essie opened her eyes and fought back a blush over the way Ross Montgomery stared with a smug smile that said he had her. *Oh, hell.* So what if he was right about her cooking? It didn't change anything. "Thank you so much for the flattery. I really do appreciate the offer, but my answer is still no."

He seemed somehow completely undisturbed by her answer, and Essie watched as he took a sip of his champagne and finished off the tart.

Then he looked up at her. "Aren't you going to have more of the mousse? I'm sorry I finished off the tart, but it's a testament to your artistry."

"No, I really should be getting back to the kitchen." She started to rise when he put his warm hand on top of hers, stilling her.

"If I could just have another moment of your time, please, Ms. Bradford?"

Essie sat back down as he seemed to assess her from top to bottom.

"How about this? Now, I know I can't make up for you not being home with your family on the holiday, but I can assure that you do get the rest, or at least some of it that you're craving. And I get our mutual friend, Misha, off my back, which, for this, you would be doing me the hugest favor."

Essie smiled. She knew how tough Misha could be when it came to her patients and friends.

Ross continued. "For this holiday I'm taking my new yacht, the *Serenity*, on a trip from New York to Miami to impress clients to invest in my new resort. This is a huge deal for me, so I can't put it off, as Misha so boldly suggested." He looked at her now and gave the corner of his lip a light lick, which was entirely too sexy. "Misha said your food was delicious, and she was absolutely right about that. She also said that you do a fine job of cooking healthy food in a new way, and you do wonders with changing your clients' lifestyles. I want you to do that for me."

Essie's whole body went on alert. In that moment there were way too many things she wanted to do for him. But she needed to focus. Get the "no" in gear. She forced herself to listen to his words and not just watch his sexy lips.

"Sadly, I usually eat on the run and I need to change that. And though I hate to admit it to Misha, I do my share of burning the candle at both ends. So if you would join me on my yacht, I'll give you great accommodations, and in exchange you'll take care of my dietary needs, take a fabulous trip, and I'll pay you handsomely."

"Mr. Montgomery, I don't think you're hearing me," Essie started, hoping she sounded more secure than she felt.

"Ms. Bradford, I don't think *you're* hearing *me.* I know your going rate, and I previously offered a five-thousand-dollar bonus, but I'm willing to make that ten thousand dollars if you take the job. And on top of that, my boat comes with another chef, so you won't be working alone to feed everyone on the trip. Your job will be mostly taking care of my dietary needs. The other chef will do all the heavy lifting. Now, will you please take the position?"

Essie was stunned. A ten-thousand-dollar signing bonus on top of her usual rate to luxuriate on a yacht and cook meals for one person? She would be crazy to say no. But how was it that he was coming to her now when she already decided her new motto was "NO"? And how could she leave her mother alone over the holiday? This would only be their second one without Dad. She should just keep to her original schedule and spend the holidays with her mother. But what would her mother say if she found out she turned this offer down? This would go so far toward her savings, and so far toward her dream of her own restaurant. Not to mention the fact that she now had to cover Cam's half of the rent. She looked back at Ross and saw a bit of a twinkle in those ridiculously gorgeous eyes.

Damn. He probably knew he had me the moment he walked in the door. "You don't have to look so smug, Mr. Montgomery. I didn't say yes, you know."

"Yet," he said. "You didn't say yes . . . yet. And don't look so pitiful about it. I'm taking you on a yacht, Ms. Bradford, not the *Titanic.*"

Essie picked up her spoon and dug into the chocolate mousse at the same time Ross did. "So should we toast with chocolate mousse?"

Ross grinned and raised his spoon. "As long as I have you on my boat next week, and in my galley, I'll toast in any way, with anything you want, Ms. Bradford."

Essie got a tingle then, where there was no place for a tingle to be given. They were now boss and employee, so she gave him a sharp look. "I would tell you to call me Essie, but since I'm now working for you, I guess we'd better stay on a last-name basis, Mr. Montgomery."

Chapter 4

"I don't know about this, Mish," Essie said into her cell as the cab made its way down the highway in the early-morning hours. The air was crisp and still gray, the sun only being hinted at as it glinted off the mirrored chrome of the New York skyscrapers.

"What's not to know? You should be thanking me," Misha replied. "I know you didn't plan to work during the holiday, but with Cam hitting the wind and you needing extra money, this is perfect. Besides, it will be good for you."

Essie could feel Misha scheming through the phone and her eyes rolled skyward. "Good for me how? Cam and I have only been broken up for less than a week."

Misha let out an impatient snort. "Oh, please. You and Cam were broken up the moment he screwed his assistant, and I'd bet that was at least two months ago, if not more. The moment you hit the road to work with the band, you two were done."

"Ouch, leave it to you not to pull any punches."

"What good would it do? Life is too short. Now you remember that while you're sailing with Ross. He'll be a tough client, but I've known him a long time, and he's a good guy underneath."

It was Essie's turn to snort. "Underneath what? The latest supermodel? Let Google tell it. He's got a deli number-counter at the foot of his bed."

Now Misha laughed. "You, more than anyone, should know that outside appearances can be deceiving. I know you're not totally the 'Little Miss Zen' you want the world to see. Now go and whip my friend into shape. Tell him I want great numbers on his next visit. And from you, I want a report that you had a fabulous time. Doctor's orders."

"Yeah, whatever you say," Essie said before switching off.

The taxi began to slow as it turned by the piers, and the most beautiful boat Essie had ever seen came into her view.

"Oh, my freaking God," she whispered as she got out of the cab, pulling her carryall in one hand and her cooking supplies in the other. Essie knew the galley would more than likely be fully stocked, and she had sent over a list of what she wanted available. But she wouldn't assume it would be stocked with her favorite organic oils, not to mention her homemade spice blends and whenever possible, she never did a job without her old faithful set of stainless pans and, of course, her knives. She paused as two crewmembers in white pants and long-sleeved black shirts appeared, their hands behind their backs, sunglasses on, watching her as she made her way.

When she was finally in front of them, the one that looked a little older, but only because of the light graying at his temples, gave a little nod and a small smile. "And I'm guessing you are Ms. Bradford. Welcome to *Serenity.*"

"Thank you, and please call me Essie." She looked up at the ship and its impressive height. "So, *Serenity*? A ship this size I expect to be called the *Enterprise.*"

The man grinned and stepped forward. "I'm Jeff Grayson,

the ship's captain, and this guy right here is Cooper Westport, our chief engineer."

Cooper smiled next to Captain Grayson, and though his sunglasses covered a good portion of his face, Essie could still tell from his thick blond hair, chiseled jaw, and his blindingly white smile that he was a good-looking man.

"Great to meet you, Essie," Cooper said with a cute Aussie accent.

More tall men in the same uniform came out and stood along the deck as Cooper made the introductions.

"That right there is my second, Ethan Chambers." Ethan gave a nod and smile. "And next to him is our deckhand Jayce Spencer." Jayce gave a slight bow and then came forward to take Essie's bags from her. "And then we have Quincy Bell, our head steward. He'll help with any personal needs you may have."

"Very nice to meet you," Quincy said. Another man with a lovely accent, this time it was from the United Kingdom.

Essie smiled and shook hands.

"You all are being so kind. I'm sure I won't need anything. I'll try and not be too much of a bother."

"I'll be the judge of that," came another new, slightly gruffer voice.

"And finally," Cooper said, his own voice now slightly apologetic, "we have Chef Simon Scott. I guess you and he will be working pretty closely together."

Essie looked toward Chef Scott, who wore shades just as the rest of the crew was, but unlike the others, his were pushed up onto the top of his clean-shaven head to reveal his sharp, assessing eyes and stern brow. And though she bestowed on him her easy smile, he countered back with nothing but a slight nod.

Fine, that's how you want to play? Essie had been in the cooking game for a long time. Chef Scott was surely not the first, and he wouldn't be the last, temperamental chef she'd come across. She'd give it a day, and she was sure they'd be getting along just fine. If not, it didn't matter. This job was only temporary. "It's very nice to meet you, Chef. I'll be in and out of your hair in no time flat," she said.

"Is that a promise, little lady?" Chef Scott stated more than asked.

Essie looked at him dead-on and stepped onto *Serenity.* "It's a statement, nothing more. I've learned early on that promises are worth no more than the breath it takes to make them."

Quincy finished giving Essie a quick tour of the ship and she was officially in awe. *Serenity* was 130 feet, four levels, and no luxury spared. There was a formal and informal salon, a gym, two hot tubs, jet skis, a diving plank, a formal dining room, as well as an informal one. By the time she got to the galley, her mouth hung open. Hell, she was thinking she should be paying Ross for this trip, but she knew she could never afford it. Not in a million years.

Quincy showed her the crew's quarters and lead her to her own room. She turned a corner too quickly and walked into a solid wall that was Ross Montgomery's chest. "Oh, my goodness, um, I'm sorry, excuse me."

"Please don't apologize, Ms. Bradford," Ross said. His large warm hands righted her, steady in the most unsteady way. "Things can get a little tight on this ship."

At his words his and Essie's eyes met, and if she were still fourteen and believed in such a thing, she'd swear fireworks went off. Essie quickly lowered her eyes and stepped back, but not before catching the laughter in Ross's eyes. *Damn.*

"I was just giving Ms. Bradford a tour, sir, and leading her to her quarters," Quincy said, breaking the unspoken tension.

"I'll take over from here, thank you," Ross said, his voice low, but still definite and commanding.

Essie watched Quincy's retreating back and, for some reason, wanted to follow him down the narrow hallway, but she knew she couldn't, so she stood where she was. "I didn't know you were on board," she said.

"Yet here I am," Ross said matter-of-factly. "I was finishing a work call when you arrived. I'm sorry I couldn't greet you. But now that you are here, we may depart."

She felt a brow shoot up. "But I thought you said this was a business trip and you were taking clients down to Florida."

"This is a business trip, but no, we're picking up clients in Florida. I hope I didn't give you the wrong impression."

Essie, relax. This isn't a big deal. It's still business and still a trip.

Just with a lot less passengers on the way down than she anticipated. It didn't matter. She wasn't here for his clients anyway. She was here to get him on track to good food and a new lifestyle. Essie brought her shoulders up and looked him in the eye. "It's no matter who is here. It's you who's paying me, and you are my client."

Essie couldn't help but notice his jaw tighten at this statement. "This is true, I am paying you, but as we discussed, you're still my guest. So, how about you let me show you to your room?" He put his arm out in a gesture for her to follow him. They climbed a narrow flight of stairs, going from below deck up another level, to where the accommodations were more spacious and, if possible, more luxurious.

Ross took Essie past some of the most sumptuous staterooms she had ever seen, all done up in marble and wood. This was a world of luxury beyond her imagination. At one point he stood outside a room and waved his hand. "These are my quarters, and my office is right next door. Since this is a working trip, I will be in my office quite a bit. Though, per Misha's orders, I promise to go above deck and get some sun while I work, from time to time."

Essie smiled. "I'll hold you to it. Do you mind if I take a look?"

"Not at all."

Essie peeked in the door of his stateroom. It was decorated in the same modern way as the rest of the yacht, but here there was a classic twist that was a little bit dressed down so that it was more casual and, somehow, more sexy. The low-profile bed had a utilitarian feel to it, and the artwork that hung over the bed was done in tones of gray, with a splash of red. The gray lamps by the bed added to the coolness of the room. The thick gray carpeting made her want to take off her shoes and sink her toes into it. Everything about the room was sensual and inviting in an ultracool way. So very much like the man himself.

Essie swallowed and looked up at Ross. "It's a cool space."

Cool? She wanted to bang herself in the head. Instead, she swallowed and gave a weak smile.

Ross's smile threatened to turn her legs to noodles. "Thanks."

He opened the door next to it to show his office. This was a continuation of his bedroom, sexy, sleek, and modern. With one wall made of all glass windows to take in the sea view.

"I hope I won't find you always in here. According to our agreement, you have to learn some things from me about food and perhaps cooking?" Essie challenged.

He frowned and closed the office door. "We'll have to see about that, Ms. Bradford."

"That we will, Mr. Montgomery."

Ross turned away from his office door and surprised her by turning to a door right across from his own. "And this will be your accommodations."

Essie stepped inside and this time she really couldn't stop her mouth from dropping open. "Oh, Ross, this is too much. I mean, Mr. Montgomery. Really, I can sleep down in the crew's quarters. They are more than generous."

She watched as his lip worked a little at the corner in amusement. "You will sleep here, Ms. Bradford, and not insult me. According to our agreement, you're not one of the crew, and though you are not one of the official guests, you are my guest, and this is your holiday, though a working one it may be. So please enjoy this room with my compliments. I won't hear any arguments."

Essie frowned, looking at the ridiculously luxurious accommodations. She had never been in a room so beautiful. It was mahogany and marble like the rest of the ship, but this was designed with a woman in mind as the décor was accented in creams and natural stone. Not to mention the beautiful orchids she spied. And in the bathroom there was both a stand-up shower and a beautiful Jacuzzi tub. After this, how would she ever go back to her small one-bedroom apartment? She looked at Ross and shook her head. "You always make it this hard for a girl to turn you down?"

"I do my very best, Ms. Bradford."

Essie let out a sigh as she eyed the huge bed. "That's what I'm afraid of, Mr. Montgomery."

Chapter 5

Ross fought the urge to retreat to his office. Instead, he went up to join the captain on the bridge. Not that he wanted to retreat to his office, or that he wanted to join the captain. No, what he really wanted to do was stay with the pretty Ms. Bradford and kiss her on that deliciously large bed until that skeptical look she kept giving him gave way to one of glazed passion.

Shit. What is wrong with me? Number one, she was now an employee, at least for the next ten days, so she should technically be off limits if his normal code of ethics applied. And number two, which was the head-scratcher, she was not his type, so he didn't get the intense, almost uncontrollable, physical attraction.

It had been there as soon as he caught a glimpse of her in the restaurant, even before he knew who she was and their eyes locked for the first time. He didn't get it. This type of thing never happened to him. He didn't believe in happenstance or anomalies out of the realm. Ross lived in absolutes. And Essie Bradford was a wild card.

She was nothing like the usual strain of models. She was tall, sure. That fit his bill. But that's where it ended. His usual women had a certain—Ross paused in his thoughts, looking for the right description, and he grimaced when all he could come up with was "body shop shine and polish" to them. It was as if the women he usually went for stepped off the showroom runway, dyed, plucked and blown out, falling that way into his bed.

But not Essie Bradford. She was tall and slim, but he could tell by her well-fitting jeans and no-nonsense sweater, she had delicious curves in all the right places. And her skin, Ross sucked in a breath, there was something about her skin, with its rich, chocolate tone that seemed to glow from deep within, made him long to touch it, taste it, be a part of it. *Freaking hell!* Even to his own mind he was already sounding whipped.

But still, her eyes came to his mind. Deep and soulful, sparking like onyx jewels, only there to enhance the full lips he wanted to kiss so very much. Those plump lips that made him think of her delicious desserts and all the ways he wanted to devour her.

Damn it! This whole thing was a huge mistake. He knew that now. Just as he knew that Misha, wherever she was, must be laughing her ass off. Ross reached the bridge and Captain Grayson turned around. "I just want to check if we're on schedule and you have everything you need."

The older man smiled and looked around at all the shiny new equipment. "I have more than I need, sir. I can't wait to get her out in the open water. It will be an honor to sail her."

Ross grinned. "Well, I'm happy to have you in charge and on board. I'm going to go up to the fly deck and watch the launch."

"Enjoy, sir. The weather is optimum, so we should be good."

Ross exited while the captain made an announcement for all hands to be ready to leave. On his way up top, Ross thought for a moment about going to collect Essie and invite her to join him, but stopped. Setup or not, he wouldn't play into Misha's hands. His life, if not his numbers, was fine as it was. And he didn't need the complications of some goody-two-shoes, interfering chef.

Really he should have invited Lela on this trip, or a version of her. It wouldn't have been hard. But something stopped him from doing that. Yes, it was a business trip, but he knew his clients. Most were married and would be bringing their wives, and those without would bring girlfriends or expect some sort of female entertainment. They all expected him to show up with a beautiful woman on his arm, as he always did. And that night at the restaurant when he first saw Essie, he was so close to inviting Lela to come with him, but he stopped and he let her go on to that sneaker party. The question was why.

Just as Ross got topside, as if by some divine answering, there was the "why" at the railing. Her face was lifted up to catch the breeze; her hair was whipping playfully, fighting the wind and losing. But still she smiled to herself, saying a silent goodbye to cold New York while *Serenity* backed away from the city. Taking her away from home and family and him away from nothing but his newly remodeled three thousand square feet of . . . now that he thought about it, way too open apartment space.

The moment filled Ross with an unexpected sense of melancholy. In his mind he saw visions of skating with his little girl, hand in hand, under the colorful lights of the Rockefeller Center Christmas Tree. Ross shook the thought off with an inward snort. Not that it would be happening. She was in California and would be enjoying the holiday as she always did, with her mother and stepdad. She was happy, and that was enough.

"The view is beautiful, isn't it?" Ross said as he eased next to Essie and leaned against the railing.

She turned slowly and faced him, as if she knew he would walk up and stand next to her. "It really is. It's been so long since I've seen New York from the water. As a kid I used to love to take the Staten Island Ferry to get this view."

Ross smiled. "I used to do that as a kid, too. Best cheap view in the city. That, and the Roosevelt Island Tram."

Essie's eyes went wide. "You're so right. I love the tram. I used to go back and forth just for the fun of it. Now that I'm over the free kid height, no more back and forth for me. Not with the way metro fares keep going up. More and more it seems the joys of the city have been priced out for regular folks." Essie averted her eyes, as if remembering she was on a yacht with a real estate developer. "I'm sorry, I didn't mean, well, you know."

"No offense taken. You don't have to be sorry for saying what you think. I agree. The city is way too expensive. And there should be simple luxuries and joys available to everyone. Now, I know that sounds crazy coming from me, with us standing on my yacht, but it's true."

Her eyes got that skeptical gleam once again. "Okay," she replied with a shrug, turning away.

Ross crossed his arms. "You don't take anything at face value, do you?"

She frowned and turned toward the city, staring a long time

before turning back to him, her expression once again a mask of calm. "That's not true. As a matter of fact, I take everything at face value. I'm the type of woman who believes what I see. I believe people show you who they are, and, as Ms. Angelou's saying goes, when they do, believe them."

She smiled brightly; then those full lips went wide and once again she showed that quirky armor-shattering space in her front teeth, which he found so endearing. But her statement said a lot. This woman had a history, and she'd also been hurt. For some reason Ross wanted to know more. He frowned then, about to question her, but she cut him off flicking her wrist and checking her watch.

"Look at the time. Quincy sent me your usual schedule and I'd like to take a little time to get to know your galley before I start to prepare lunch. Do you have anything you absolutely don't like?"

Knowing this was the end of that particular conversation, Ross relented. "Never been a fan of asparagus or Brussels sprouts."

"I'll make note of that, sir."

Ross frowned.

"What is it? Is it something else?"

"I also don't appreciate you calling me 'sir.'"

"Why? I've noticed everyone else does aboard the ship."

"Well, you're not everyone else. You're working for me, but we've established we have a special situation, and since we share a mutual friend, can we, once and for all, get on a first-name basis and get a little less formal?" Ross didn't know why he made this little speech. Maybe it was the way she held her arms so tightly together, or maybe it was the rigidity of her spine, or the way she tilted her chin up at him. But all he wanted in that moment was for her to soften her stance at least a little bit. If all he could do was get it in a name, then so be it.

It was crazy, he knew. But somehow looking at her, and the way she looked at him, Ross knew respect was not what he wanted from her. He wanted something different, something more. Something strangely close to admiration, approval, or maybe something even more dangerous. Something like affection.

Essie gave him that weary look once again, and then her eyes went soft at the same time something on him went dangerously hard. *Oh, hell.* She stuck out her hand and smiled. "I'm Essie. Nice to meet you."

Ross's lips quirked, feeling shy, an emotion he definitely didn't welcome. He took her hand in his, enjoying the feel of its powdery coolness. "I'm Ross. It's nice to meet you, too."

Essie's eyes narrowed as she pulled her hand from his, leaving him feeling slightly bereft. "Okay, I'm going to give you a warning. Now that we're officially friends, there will be no holding back from me. I'm going to be as tough on you as Misha would be. Today starts the rest of your life. So remember you asked for it."

Ross watched as Essie made her way from the deck and disappeared going toward the galley. "Don't worry, Essie. I'm sure I'll enjoy every moment."

Chapter 6

Every moment? What the hell does he mean by every moment?

Essie made her way to the galley, wondering if Ross knew she'd heard his parting comment, and happily only getting turned around twice, which she attributed to the size of the boat and not her "Ross infatuation." Freaking Misha. Sure, he would be enjoying every moment. He had a silly chef who mooned over his broad shoulders and smooth handsomeness at every turn. What was there *not* to enjoy?

Get your crap together, girl. None of her usual emotion-filled, wear-your-heart-on-your-sleeve ways. She had to be strong. She'd been burned one too many times by smooth-talking men to take anything they said at more value than playing a game, or playing her. She'd gone on long enough listening to her heart. It was the head's turn to lead. And as for listening to regions farther south, which seemed to be blaring horns and trumpets when Ross Montgomery was in spitting distance, she was putting that area on mute, as it was not to be relied on for good advice.

When Essie got to the kitchen, Chef Scott was leaning against the counter, arms folded as if he was standing guard over his domain.

She smiled. "Hello, Chef. Once again, I hope you don't mind me butting in on your domain. I'll try my best to stay out of your way, but I may ask for a little help from you, as I'm new to finding out what Ross"—Essie paused—"I mean, Mr. Montgomery likes, and I've been charged to convert his diet to something a bit more heart healthy."

She watched as the already-rigid chef drew his body even tighter and stood taller, while plumping his chest out.

"Do you mean to tell me there is something wrong with my food? Are you trying to say there's something unhealthy about it?"

"Of course not," Essie soothed. "I'm sure your food is top-notch, or there is no way you would have been hired to be the head chef on such an exclusive boat. I was brought on as a nutritionist and a consultant. My expertise has nothing to do with your capability. Like I was saying, I'm sure there's plenty I can learn from you."

"Oh, what do I care about how he spends his money? You are just another in a long line of more of the same."

Essie bristled, but refused to bite, keeping her smile, but lowering her tone. "You're right. It is his money, and I suggest you do your job, and start by showing me around the kitchen and pantry properly. I want to be sure the items I listed to be supplied are all accounted for."

She and Chef Scott stared at each other, and once again Essie was up against a man she knew she could not back down from. But just when she thought he was about to break, a voice came from over her shoulder. "Why are you not moving, Simon? Like you said, it's my money. What? Are you afraid you may learn something?" Both Essie and the chef turned around at the sound of Ross's voice.

"I . . . I didn't mean anything by it, sir," Chef Scott stammered out.

Ross gave him a steely stare. "Let's be sure you didn't, because if you did, I can easily find other ways to spend my money than on your paycheck."

"Why, yes, sir, of course."

Essie saw the bloom of embarrassment take over the chef's face and a hint of anger as he clenched his jaw.

"Ross, really, it's all fine. Chef Scott and I were having a discussion about working arrangements. This is his kitchen, and he was showing me around."

Ross shot her a look that was at once caring, but somehow dismissive, and the smile he gave her didn't quite reach his eyes. "Now, in all actuality it's my kitchen." He turned to Chef Scott. "Am I right?"

The chef gave a nod of his head as his eyes went downcast. "That you are, and as you said, I'm sure there's plenty for me to learn."

Ross nodded then and smiled. It was that sexy and somehow dangerous smile that made Essie want to step away from him, when, at the same time, she wanted to step forward into his atmosphere.

He clasped his hands together, casually breaking the serious mood. "Well, then, I'll leave you both to it. Essie, I can't wait to taste what you have in store for me this afternoon."

As he left, Chef Scott lowered his hands and let out an audible sigh. Then he shot Essie a look that, while full of disdain, showed his defeat. "You heard the man. This is his boat, his home, and, as of now, it looks like you're the lady of the house." He made a wide gesture with his arms. "What's mine is now yours. So please tell me, how can I be of service to you?"

Chapter 7

Though Ross was deep in conversation with his lawyer, he somehow felt Essie's presence outside his office door, even before she gave it a knock. "Hold on a minute, Barry. Come in," Ross said.

As Essie entered, Ross felt his body, his entire body, immediately spring to attention, like a trained Pavlovian dog. He couldn't help but notice the look of surprise she tried to hide at seeing the mess his office had become in the short time he'd been working. He was a bit of a manic worker and liked to spread things out, so just about every available surface was covered. There was no place for her to set the tray.

He watched as she did a little spin, which showed off her figure nicely, but as she came up empty, she turned back to him in frustration. "Barry, I'm going to have to get back to you. I'll call you in a half an hour or so." Ross cut off his call without waiting for a reply and got up from his seat.

Essie gave him a quick glare. "You didn't have to do that. I need a place to put the tray, and then I'll go so you can work."

"Who said I was hanging up for you? Presumptuous, aren't we, Ms. Bradford?" Ross gave Essie a grin. And he got back a hard stare.

"Not at all. I thought we agreed we were on a first-name basis, Ross. Now, do you care to let me know where to put the tray? It's getting pretty heavy."

Ross ran over and cleared space on the seating area's coffee table. He then took the tray out of Essie's hands, and fought to ignore the little spark of electricity that sizzled through him when their fingertips grazed. He had no time for shivers or sparks. He had a deal to get done, despite what Misha's plans for him were.

"Thank you. I hope you enjoy it."

Shit. Even her voice gave him shivers. All sweet and full of sass, but still with a hint of honey, even though she seemed mad as all get-out. "I'm sure I will. Now, tell me what it is. And while you're at it, you can tell me why you're ready to spit nails at me." Ross took a seat on the couch and lifted the cover on the plate, giving it a look over.

His eyes popped up when Essie cleared her throat. "Lunch is a simple ratatouille. Eggplant, bell peppers, onions, zucchini, some tomatoes, all served over quinoa. And for dessert you've got a seasonal fruit plate with a vinaigrette dressing."

Ross looked over the tray and frowned.

"What's the matter?"

Ross gestured for Essie to take one of the chairs and watched as she seemed to do a double take before taking a seat, as if the chair would bite her or something.

"Okay. I'm sitting. What's wrong? I'm here to serve you."

Ross couldn't help his raised brow at that last comment, and still she was as taut as a fully loaded slingshot. "Are you going to tell me what has you so stiff-lipped and fired up?"

"I don't think I'm being stiff," she said. "But what is slightly bothersome to me is the fact that I didn't need you butting in when I was hashing things out with Chef Scott."

Ross was quiet. It wasn't as if she was wrong. He had been high-handed, but a guy like Simon needed to be pulled in, and pulled in quick, otherwise he could get out of hand. "I apologize for that. But as I said, this is my vessel, and I know Simon's reputation. He can be a bit of a bully, and you are my guest. I wanted to make that clear, so he wouldn't think anything otherwise. I will apologize, though. I don't want to make you feel uncomfortable in any way. If it was any other situation, I would let you handle it yourself. But since you're my guest, I felt it was my duty to step in."

Essie's lips tightened. He could tell she didn't like his high-handedness, but, hopefully, she couldn't fault his logic. She looked over at Ross as he was eyeing the green smoothie.

"I see you are frowning. Is there something wrong with your lunch?"

Ross looked up, slightly bewildered. "There's no chocolate." He searched the tray again. "None of your chocolate puff pastry, chocolate tart, not even a hint of my favorite, your chocolate mousse."

Essie gave him a long look before speaking slowly, as if he were a child. "First of all, man cannot live on chocolate alone."

"So say you, but I beg to differ."

Essie let out a snort, but at least he got a hint of a smile. "As I was saying, man should not live by chocolate alone. And how was I to know that you wanted it at every meal? Is that why you hired me, for my chocolate?"

His brow shot up and she blushed. A distinct rosiness radiated under her deep brown skin. She knew she walked right into that one, and it was cute as hell. Essie shook her head. "Really, Ross. Grow up. Besides, Misha would have my ass. There is no way she would sanction that sort of diet for you."

"Why? It's not like I need to lose weight. I'm in great physical shape."

Essie looked him over then, and with her dark, assessing gaze, his old jeans and sweater suddenly felt about two sizes too tight.

"Okay, I'll give you that," she finally said. "You can have a bit of chocolate, but you need to up your fruit, too."

He grinned at a small victory, then frowned again. "And I'm not really a fan of quinoa."

"Please don't tell me my newest client is a five-year-old. Misha warned me your taste in food was somewhat"—Essie paused—"shall I say, juvenile?"

"Hey, just because I like a burger now and again doesn't make my tastes juvenile."

"Fine. But if those burgers are from a fast-food restaurant that you've had your driver pull up to more than three times a week, I'd call that *juvenile.*"

Ross gave her a hard stare and she gave him one in return. He blinked and Essie grinned, no doubt enjoying her moment of victory.

"You know, nobody who works for me gives me so much grief."

"Why am I feeling that nobody gives you grief if they work for you or not? Now pick up your fork and eat your lunch like a good CEO."

Ross shook his head and did as he was told. Essie smiled, clearly enjoying the fact he was enjoying her food. She took pride in her work and he could respect that. For so long with him it always seemed to be about the bottom line, just numbers on a page. But when was the last time he really looked at the work he was doing? Took time to look and enjoy all he'd built?

"What is it now?" Essie asked.

He looked her in the eye, enjoying the moment of getting lost in their depths. "Nothing at all. This lunch is terrific, Chef."

She grinned a wholly satisfied grin, which was nothing short of glorious on her.

"Well done. You can stop gloating. You know you did great."

"You caught me. Later we'll talk breathing and maybe some meditation?"

At that, Ross let out a growl and Essie chuckled as she got up to make her exit. "Okay, I won't push my luck. At least not for today. I'll see you at dinner. Don't work too hard."

"Don't worry, I always do."

As Ross watched Essie's retreating back, and then headed back toward the phone, he was surprised by how much he enjoyed the banter with Essie. He couldn't remember the last time he had fun simply talking to a woman, or anyone for that matter, about a subject that wasn't business related. With her, talking came easy. And now as he picked up his phone and looked at the closed door, he found himself already looking forward to dinner and their next conversation.

Chapter 8

Essie was laying out the dough for her puff pastries when Quincy came in with Ross's discarded tray. "Well, it would seem your first lunch was a hit, Ms. Bradford."

Essie grinned. "That's good to hear, and please call me Essie."

Quincy reached over and nabbed a strawberry from her bowl. "And you can call me Quince. So, what brings you here to sail away with our little crew?" Quincy made an exaggerated fanning motion. "You know, besides the fact that our fearless leader is the hottest eligible bachelor on the planet?"

Essie's head shot up from her work. "That is definitely not the reason I'm here. I'm here to cook, and that's about it. Just doing a favor for a friend."

"Oh, my dear. You must have some really good friends. I need to hang with a better class of people," Quincy said with a laugh.

Essie laughed along with him as Ethan, the bosun, came in, followed by Jayce, the deckhand, who lifted his T-shirt to wipe at his sweaty brow, despite the chill of the sea air outside. Essie averted her gaze, but not before checking out his rippled abs. She bit back a giggle as she fought down a blush.

"Oh, darling, you have a lot to learn about us guys at sea. We are one big happy family on this boat," Quincy teased, catching her look.

Cooper came over and gave her shoulder a squeeze. His crystal blue eyes sparkled with sweet charm. "That's right, E."

She grinned, already liking her new nickname.

"We all get along like peas in a pod here. All for one, and one for all. Those are the rules." He dipped his pointer finger into her bowl of chocolate and took a long lick. "This is delicious!" He looked at his mates. "Guys, this woman's food is as sweet as she looks. We've got a winner here."

Essie gave him a smile along with a playful shove. "Watch those hands, Cooper. And definitely no double dipping."

"All right, boys, that's enough," came Ross's deep voice, stopping all conversation like a scratched record. "No dipping your fingers into my bowl without permission." At the double entendre no one knew whether to laugh or not, so it was Essie who broke the tension, refusing to let Ross once again come into the kitchen and ruin what she was trying to build.

"You'd better be talking about these stainless-steel bowls, because if not, you'll be meeting the hard end of one of my frying pans."

Ross stepped down from the stairs and fully into the galley. Everyone was silent as Ross and Essie stared at each other. He raked his eyes from her eyes to her lips, down to her breasts and on to her hands, back up to her lips, then her eyes again. Each point he hit seemed to flame along his route. "Now, what else could I possibly be referring to?" he finally growled out before walking over to the fridge and pulling out a beer, twisting the cap and taking a pull.

"Sir, I could have brought that to you," Quincy spoke up.

He gave Quincy an exasperated look. "I'm not helpless, Quince. But what you can do for me is prepare the small dining room." He then looked at Essie again. "If you wouldn't mind joining me there for dinner, Ms. Bradford?"

Oh, boy, so bowls licked and they were back to that. Essie gave him a cool smile. "Sure, Mr. Montgomery. I'll see you at eight."

The smile she got in return before he walked off could have frozen the water they sailed on, but she ignored it and continued her work. She wouldn't let him get to her. No way was he ruining her mood or her food.

Essie finished her work, filled her pastries, and then handed Cooper the spoon.

He laughed at that. "Oh, E, you are a tough one."

"Of course I'm not. You said it yourself. I'm as sweet as my chocolate, and don't let anybody tell you different."

Chapter 9

The petite dining salon might as well have been called the grand salon for all its opulence. The wood of the table was polished to a high shine as was the modern glass chandelier above with its golden accents. Not to mention the china was also gold edged and gleaming. Quincy had done a beautiful job with the settings. *Maybe a little too beautiful,* Essie thought as she caught the reflections of the candlelight in the large windows, which offered a beautiful view of the glistening moonlight bouncing off the dark sea.

Crap, this is looking a little too much like a date! It had Essie feeling uneasy. First, about how her meal would be received, which was ridiculous because she was always confident in her food. But after seeing this setup, she was really nervous over the fact she'd be sitting and sharing a meal with Ross.

Alone.

For the first time.

Butterflies started to flutter, threatening to swirl in an uncomfortably familiar way in her belly. This was silly; she had to get it together. It wasn't a "date" date; it was Essie and a client sharing a meal.

That was it. She'd consider it an assignment.

But as she was laying out her dishes in the center of the table, and removing her chef's smock to reveal the simple black cotton dress underneath, Ross walked in, looking like 110 percent of movable sex and money in his slacks, high-shined shoes, and expensive dress shirt. The butterflies went wild.

Essie brushed at her bangs and tugged on her casual dress, which now felt like an old painter's smock. "Sorry, I didn't have anything particularly dressy to wear. I really only came with more casual work clothes and these easy dresses." *Oh, God, why am I explaining myself to this man? Shut up, Essie.*

Ross smiled as he walked over to her. His closeness and clean freshly showered scent, with a hint of some expensive undertone, sent her senses into overdrive as he pulled out the chair for her. The urge to lean over and lick his neck was overwhelming.

"You look absolutely perfect."

Oh, hell, if that wasn't the worst thing he could have said. The butterflies went into a tailspin as her hormones followed behind.

In that moment Essie longed to be in the crew dining area, enjoying a casual laugh-it-up dinner with them. The safe kind, like she'd had with the band. Nothing felt casual or safe about tonight. With her out of her chef's smock, and him looking at her like he saw entirely too much, this dinner had her up front and out of the kitchen—very much on display as Essie. *Just as Essie.* She didn't like it one bit.

Thankfully, Quincy came in with the wine. "Sir, tonight we have a Pinot Noir, and I believe it will complement your meal beautifully."

Ross gave Quincy a nod as he continued his intense scrutiny of Essie. "And what is the meal for the evening?"

Essie let out a breath, which she realized she'd been holding way too long. Finally they were in her wheelhouse and she could be herself. Essie put on her best serene smile. "Well, we're starting with a pear, arugula, and warm goat-cheese salad. Then for the main dish we have sea scallops with light lemon reduction and spinach. And for dessert you'll be happy to know I've made your own mini chocolate mousse." When she spoke the word "mousse," she gave him a wink and was rewarded with a smile that was as sweet as a kid's at Christmas.

"It all looks wonderful. Can we start with the dessert?"

Essie laughed. "Oh, my goodness. I think I had it right. Deep down you are five years old."

She noticed Quincy smirk as he finished his pour and discreetly left the room.

Ross gave her that quirky brow of his. "You know you are going to ruin my reputation with my crew."

Essie reached over and began to plate the food for him. "Somehow I doubt that. No matter how much I tease, you'll find a way to wash away any bit of playfulness."

Ross took the plate and looked up at her. "Are you trying to imply that I'm no fun?"

Essie finished plating her own meal, sat down, and looked across at Ross. "I'm just saying that I call things as I see them, which I explained to you earlier, and so far all I'm seeing you do is work and be slightly scolding to your crew."

"And all I see you doing is being highly judgmental toward me. So by your logic, I can surmise that your whole world revolves around cooking and judging people." Ross took a bite of the salad and closed his eyes to let the dressing's flavors flood his senses. He gave her a smile. "One of which you're very good at"—but then he shrugged his shoulders—"the other, not so much."

Essie frowned and began to eat her meal in silence. *What does he know? Though he does have right the part about me cooking well.* The man had excellent taste when it came to food and chefs. But, hey, she was a pretty good judge of people. Essie paused in her thinking as Cam came to mind, and the waste of time and space. Roger before him. It's just she wasn't the best judge of boyfriends. So what if every time she thought she found Mr. Right, give or take a few months or few weeks, they always turned out to be Mr. Wrong. Oh, well, hell! Maybe Ross was right and she was too quick to judge, and judged in the wrong direction.

Which was why she was over trusting her "yes"; from now on, caution was the way to go.

Essie stared at Ross. He looked every bit like a bite of sweet, sexy chocolate heaven as he ate his meal. Maybe giving up her "yes" was hasty. But there was no way she was going all in and giving up her heart for a man, when all it would take was a little taste to satisfy her need.

Essie smiled to herself as she took a sip of her wine.

"You look quite content there. It's like you've had a full-on internal powwow without me. I'm starting to feel slighted. Penny for your thoughts?"

Essie stared at him for a few beats and then looked around the opulent dining room. It was lovely, but void of any personal touches. So very different from the way she lived. Thoughts of home and her mom came to her mind, and she wondered what her mother must be doing right now. Probably pulling out their old artificial Christmas tree. But would she really want to do it alone? Sadness swept through Essie in a sudden wave. "You know you can afford to pay way more than a penny for my thoughts."

Ross's lips quirked up. It was like a switch went off with that little quirk, the way her nipples hardened and the shiver sizzled down her spine.

"You're right I can pay more, but how about you share anyway. You were far away for a moment there."

She looked at him and took another sip of wine. "I was thinking about my mother for a moment and what she must be doing right now."

"And what might that be?" he asked, seeming genuinely interested.

Essie briefly considered the time. "I was thinking tonight she'd be putting up the Christmas tree, but I'm wondering if she would have wanted to do it without me. I should have made time to do it with her before I left. It's our favorite thing." Essie smiled, wanting to lighten the mood. "If she's not into tree trimming, I'm guessing, given the time, she's watching her favorite show on TV, with her feet up, having something warm to eat. Probably a leftover stew of some sort from Sunday. My mother always likes to make large pots so she doesn't have to cook during the week, since she still works fulltime at the post office."

"And what does your father do?" Ross asked.

Essie's shoulders tensed as the usual ache settled in her chest. "He drove, boy did he drive." As she heard her voice start to fade off, Essie forced herself to snap back. "He passed away two years ago," she said quickly, and then tried to cover it with a smile she hoped was bright enough. "But my mom is up for retirement soon, and I'm looking forward to taking her away on a long-awaited and much-deserved vacation one of these Christmases."

"I'm really sorry. I didn't mean to bring up a subject that would cause you pain." His voice was low and deep, full of so much sincerity that it made her pause and swallow down a lump in her throat.

Essie waved a hand across her face in dismissal. "Oh, it's fine, really. It's been a couple of years. It's just that, well, my mother and I have never been apart during the holidays, so I do worry about her being alone. But she won't really be alone. My aunt Viv invited her to come and visit with her family, so as long as there are no big fights between her and Aunt Viv between now and Christmas"—Essie rolled her eyes—"all will be fine."

Essie wanted desperately to get the subject off her and on to anything else. She noticed Ross's plate was empty and laughed. "I see you hated tonight's meal. How about we get started on dessert?" She stood to move his plate to the side buffet, when he reached out a hand to still her, and the charge was instantaneous. She turned and stared.

"I'm sorry I took you away from your mom on Christmas. You sit, and I'll move these."

Essie sat, but only because she was more stunned by this apology than anything else. She watched silently as he moved the plates to the buffet and then came back to top off her glass of wine. She looked up at him with a half smile. "I hope you aren't trying to get me drunk."

"You say that as if I would need to."

Part of Essie wanted to call him a "cocky asshole" for that comment, but his matter-of-fact way of stating it held no arrogance, and hell, it wasn't like he was lying. He was hot as sin and definitely wouldn't need to get her drunk to get her into bed. So Essie watched as he expertly served the mousse from the left and took his seat.

"You do this like you've had your fair share of practice. Have you ever worked in a restaurant?"

"As I said before, you, Essie, are quick to judge, and yes, I have."

Essie furrowed her brows. "But I looked you up. Your family is quite rich."

She saw his mouth harden a bit. "That's my family—though I did get a good amount of money when my mother passed away."

"I'm really sorry," she said, but he continued to talk, wanting to gloss over his lost parent in the same way she had.

"Don't worry. It's been even more years for me than you. And my father has not always been that forthcoming with sharing his wealth. I will say he was right in wanting me to learn all facets of business, though. I worked a few summers in the kitchens of his resorts. I did kitchen, grounds, hospitality, as well as working construction. I've seen every aspect of the business while working through college. He made sure to let me know my education would not come free."

Essie studied Ross closely and was careful with her words. "He sounds like a tough man. Are you close?"

Ross picked up his wineglass and drained it before looking at her. "That we are not. I always seem to fall just short of Dad's expectations. No matter, though. I've ceased looking for my father's approval and now only seek to satisfy myself." Ross smiled, his eyes seemingly quite far away before he blinked and his gaze turned warm and approving. "And I will say, right now I am quite satisfied."

Part of her wanted to blush and possibly preen under his approving gaze, but something in her wanted to go back to what he was clearly trying to cover up. "You have me at a loss right now, Ross. For all the judging you say I do, I can't quite figure you out. What I know from Misha is pretty much stats. That you're a hard worker, maybe overly so, and you have poor eating habits, though not the worst I've ever seen. But you counter that with hard, grinding workouts that are just as hard as your work ethic. With you, it seems to be all or nothing. For some reason Misha speaks very highly of you. I've known her for quite a while and she doesn't speak so highly of that many people, so that makes me wonder why."

Ross shrugged. "Of course Misha likes me. What's there not to like? I have that kind of effect on women."

Essie narrowed her eyes. "Yeah, I don't think so. I've known Misha a long time. She would tell me if that was the case. Either way, I think there's a little something more to you, too. What's the real reason you're working so hard that you end up in the ER, having a panic attack that scares you enough to fear it's a heart attack? What are you running from, Ross Montgomery?"

With that question Ross got up and took her hand, pulling her into his arms. His embrace was swift, but not so fast that she couldn't push back if she wanted.

But she didn't want to.

She wanted to stay where she was, her body flush against his solid hardness. Ross looked down, his dark eyes meeting her own in a challenge as old as time.

"Maybe I'm not running from anything, sweet Essie, but running toward something? Did you ever stop to think of that?"

The question took her breath away because she hadn't thought of it. She blinked in the wonderment of it all, yet at the same time she steeled herself against the emotional onslaught as his lips came down toward hers.

Quincy walked back into the dining room, breaking the sexually charged tension. "How are we doing here?" he said brightly, and stopped short when he realized what he'd walked in on.

"Oh, I'm sorry. I'll go and, uh, get you another bottle."

Essie attempted to back away, but Ross, unfazed by the interloper, kept his arm firmly around her waist and challenged her with his gaze.

"Yes, you can, Quincy," Ross said, cool as ice. "Thank you. I think we'll have it in the main deck's salon."

"Very good, sir," Quincy said as he quickly left the dining room.

"I think it would be nice to continue this conversation where we can enjoy a view of the sea."

"Why did you do that?" Essie asked, trying hard to keep a tight rein on her temper. "You may not care about what others think of you, but I sure care what they think of me."

He seemed to study her hard after that statement, making her increasingly uncomfortable under his critical eye.

"Maybe that's your problem."

Essie's gaze sharpened. "What are you talking about? I don't have a problem. Besides, it's you I'm here to fix. It's you with the problems."

He raised a brow. "If you say so, Essie."

Essie pulled back sharply, yanking herself from his embrace, then hating the decision as soon as the coolness of the broken contact hit her. "I say so."

"Methinks the lady protests just enough to try and convince herself," he said, smooth and easy. "What are you trying to do? Do you think if you play nice and be a good little girl the world will reward you? I've got news for you—it doesn't work that way. It's eat or be eaten. You're a chef. You should know that. Survival of the fittest, and all that. But Lord knows there are opportunities for a swift ass kicking around every corner."

Ross took a dangerous and altogether too-alluring step toward her as Essie fought to slow her rapidly beating heart. He was just above her, so close that she could feel his breath against her lips.

He spoke again. "But if you're smart, you'll also grab swiftly to any chance of pleasure you can get. I know I do."

Essie snorted, her mind going to him in the ER. "Yeah, and look where it's gotten you."

Ross got a dark smolder in his eye, his expression taking on a look of pure sex. "Yeah, look where it's gotten me. The question is, where will it take you?"

Essie swallowed as Ross stared at her, then gave his head a small shake as if he were dismissing her and the idea that she could be like him: a person who could swim with the big fish and hold her own. The type who could know herself and, really and truly, live in her own pleasure, come what may with the consequences.

Essie studied the idea for a moment. *Could I?* God, in that moment she really wanted to do so. All she wanted to do was to take Ross with both hands and taste all he had to offer. At least for this moment. But how could she? She barely knew him beyond two conversations, a Google search, and a friend's recommendation. Jumping into bed like that was definitely not her style. Not to mention, she was in a business relationship with him. Ten days later and maybe, yes, fine, they could go on a date and see where things went. But now? No, it couldn't be done. It shouldn't be done.

Still, Essie couldn't help the small twinge of satisfaction she got from seeing Ross's eyes widen when she surprised him by suddenly reaching up and fisting his shirt in her hands and, against all her better judgment and his presumptions, pulling him down into a kiss.

Chapter 10

Holy hell, could this woman kiss!

Ross was instantly swept away by the sweet, decadent, and surprisingly addictive taste of Essie Bradford.

Where he thought she would be timid and demure, she proved him wrong by taking charge, pulling him down to her with two hands, and rising up to meet his lips forcefully with her own. And what a first meeting it was. Those full, ripe, pillowy lips were everything he dreamed they would be. Soft and luxurious, sweet to the taste, the first touch had the normally unflappable Ross just about going weak in the knees.

But he steeled himself. Telling himself to be strong and not to lose it too quickly. Giving himself a pep talk, not unlike he did when he was a teenage boy. Think baseball stats, cold showers, bespectacled librarians . . . okay, maybe not librarians. But still, how was it this almost-unassuming woman, a chef to cook his meals, could come in here and, with a mere brush of her lips, just about lay him flat? Ross closed his eyes and let the feeling take him away.

He felt Essie's excitement as she pushed her soft body against his and her rapid heartbeat vibrated against his chest, giving him a rock-hard hard-on. She tilted her head and leaned in, going further with her kiss, tentatively easing her tongue out, to run along the seam of his lips. He was only too happy to open his own lips to let her in to taste him fully for the first time.

But with a dangerous first taste, his own emotions went out of control and Ross wrapped his arms around her body and pulled her in tight. His hands traveled down to cup her curvy bottom and pull her up against his hard erection. His tongue snaked out hungrily to taste the sweet wine and chocolate as it clung to her very clever tongue.

He wanted to taste her everywhere, to see if the sweetness continued all the way down her body. As the kiss changed, Ross took control, moving down her neck, pausing to lick along her delicate collarbone. Ross couldn't help but smile when she sighed, and his erection jumped in response to the erotic sound as it escaped her lips and her head lulled back in unabashed pleasure. That's all he wanted to do. Give her pleasure from now until the sun came up, and then do it all over again and again and again. Getting her to sigh could easily turn into a life's mission for him.

Ross reached a hand up and cupped Essie's breast and she drew in a quick inhale. Something in the quick indrawn breath pulled his attention up to her face. Seeing her beautiful dark neck thrown back in submission, her lips swollen from their passionate kiss, her eyes fluttering in dark ecstasy, about did him in. He could have her right now if he wanted. Just like so many women before, he could have her.

And then what?

Ross frowned at the unwanted question. It was one he hadn't thought of in a long time, causing him to draw back ever so slightly, breaking contact only a minuscule bit. But that bit was long enough and Essie's eyes fluttered open, looking at him with the question he asked himself, unsaid but reflected there.

And then what?

"I think I should forgo the second bottle of wine and go up to bed. Or is it down to bed?"

When Essie stepped back, she left Ross feeling more alone than he cared to admit.

"Besides, it's starting to get late and it's been a long day. How about we pick up again tomorrow? I'd like to prepare for the day and really get you started on your regime."

Letting her go anywhere, especially to bed tonight without him, was the last thing Ross wanted to do, but he wouldn't push her any further. Besides, she was right. It had been a long day. Maybe what they both needed was a little space and perspective. Also, Ross didn't want any woman to feel pressure to end up in his bed. That was a strictly-by-choice situation, always had been and always would be.

Ross cleared his throat and hoped his words came out even, and the turmoil he secretly felt was hidden. "You're right, it has been a long day. Thank you so much for dinner, it was wonderful. Misha was correct. You are a very talented chef, and I look forward to all you have in store for me during the rest of this trip."

After what they had just shared, he didn't quite know how to end the evening, which made him feel like a damn fool, since he usually knew what to do in just about every situation, especially when it came to women.

Thankfully, the surprising Essie once again took matters into her own hands and gave him an easy smile. "I'm glad you enjoyed the meal, though you will be a challenge, and I have to think of ways to counteract all the chocolate you're going to demand."

At his raised brow they both laughed.

"Don't start, Ross, just say good night. I'm going to go make sure everything is fine in the kitchen, and then I'm heading to bed. You gave me enough to think about for one day and night," she said as she casually walked off toward the galley, leaving Ross with nothing better to do than take a chilly but welcome walk along the outer deck to hopefully cool his heated passion.

It took all of one point five seconds into the new day for the night before to come flooding back to Essie's mind.

Oh, God, did I really do what I know I did?

She wanted to cringe over the embarrassment of the shameless, brazen way she came on to Ross, but at the same time she couldn't fully regret kissing him. She so wanted to give herself a high five and the "atta, girl" she knew her girlfriends would.

Essie stretched, surprised at how comfortably she had slept when she finally did drift off. *Serenity* was just that: a sure ride that cut the ocean smoothly, its engines a low hum, combined with the sensual tingle she received from Ross, sent her to sleep way more contentedly than she'd expected.

Essie went to the large window and saw the sun just coming up over the horizon, beautiful soft shades of orange where it met the still-slumbering sea. Essie longed to be outside, to smell the sea air.

She changed into her workout clothes of leggings and a tank top and grabbed her yoga mat to take her morning practice above deck.

On the way out she purposely closed her stateroom door softly so as not to wake Ross as she slipped past his door. According to the schedule, she had an hour before she had to start to prepare breakfast and then she had all day to deal with Ross and what happened last night. Before Essie went to bed, she mulled it over in her mind numerous times, and still had yet to come up with how she would handle this new facet of their equally new relationship. All she had come up with was to take it slow and continue to be a professional.

Which, to her ears, sounded quite dull.

The only voice she could hear over her own was Misha's, and it was telling her to let loose and enjoy herself. She needed this.

Cam had left her, high and dry, and this was supposed to be her holiday—a working one that it was, but still her holiday. Not to mention it had been over two months since she'd had sex. Not a desert, but bordering on a parched spell for sure. Why not let go and see where these days with Ross could take her? Why not say yes, for once, to herself and to what she wanted?

But just as she was on her way out to head to the outer deck, sure of herself and her decision, Essie heard grunting and a constant *thwacking* sound as she passed the gym. There was Ross, looking like he had been working out for at least the past hour, glistening, rich brown and drenched in sweat. He pounded hard at the heavy bag. Essie instantly felt her body go on full alert as she took in his stance. Sure-footed and strong, his arms were muscular and powerful; his loose-fitting shorts were barely being held up by the tie at his trim waist. His wide back and broad shoulders were well accented by his wet tank. When he punched the bag again, and she watched those muscles contract and release, Essie couldn't help but let out a breathy sigh.

Ross stopped and turned around, meeting her, eye to eye. "Good morning." His voice was strong and raspy. Essie could tell he was fighting to catch his breath.

"You going a bit hard for so early in the morning, aren't you?"

Ross's eyes raked over her body, and in that moment Essie could practically feel his hands grazing over her skin. He stopped briefly at her yoga mat and then came up to her eyes with a playful smile. "And I see you like to take things slow and easy in the morning. Duly noted."

Essie's eyes narrowed. "Here it is, the sun is barely up, and you are spoiling for an argument."

"With you, Ms. Bradford, I'd hit the mat anytime, any way."

Essie smiled, then looked at the fairly large, cleared workout area in the exercise room. It could easily accommodate a yoga session for two. She looked back at Ross with a challenge in her eyes. "Okay, Mr. Montgomery. Just be sure you remember you said that. The session starts now."

Ross was only too happy to oblige. He loved to shake her up. Liked to see that little spark of fire she got when they sparred a bit and he called her Ms. Bradford. She really had no idea how hot she was. And time in a possible downward-dog position with the delectable Essie Bradford? He'd be a fool to hesitate.

Eagerly, he took off his sneakers and let her place him in

position on the mat. Her strong but gentle fingers at his waist instantly put his body on alert, reminding him of the fact that thoughts of her put him through a tortured and restless night.

It wasn't so easy making it through this workout. Ross spent most of his time torn between wanting to look at her beautifully shaped form in her work-out gear, and fighting looking at said form because of the effects on his body.

He took the edge off by going tried and true, thinking of sports, stocks, anything but her shapely figure. Thankfully, Essie wasn't easy on him. Starting out slow and easy, after a while picking up the pace, taking him through a series of moves that had him panting for air like he did with his cross-fit trainer back home. When she was down in a sort of modified plank and swooped into a cobra and quickly went from there—back to plank, then up into some mad one-armed twisted-pretzel thing—all Ross could do was lean back and marvel at her strength as his own muscles cried "uncle."

Essie gracefully came out of position and gave him a saucy wink. "You've had enough?"

"I may regret saying this, but yes. I give up. You got the best of me this morning, Essie." For his acquiescence, Ross was rewarded with a smile so sweet that he suddenly felt like he could do twenty laps around the deck and not break a sweat.

"Okay," she said, her voice going low, taking on a softer tone. "How about we relax and cool down for a minute. Just stretch and breathe before we really start the day?"

She took him through an easy series of floor stretches and some light breathing, only to test his willpower to the max when, in order to get his legs stretched wider apart, she used her own outstretched legs to open his. "Are you trying to be the death of me, woman?" he asked, giving her a look that left no question as to what he was really talking about.

But Essie played it cool, taking his hands in hers, and giving him a tug forward toward her most intimate of places. "I'm only trying to challenge you. Make sure you're getting all you paid for."

He leaned back, gently pulling her forward toward him. "There are some things I never pay for."

At that, she stilled, and there they were for the moment—both suspended, legs spread, hand in hand, eye to eye, both wanting the same thing, but pulling in opposite directions.

There was a noise from the gym doorway, a discreet cough that had both their heads turning. Quincy.

"Once again, Quincy, your timing is perfect."

Quincy was impeccable, despite the early hour and the embarrassing moment of the night before. "That it is, sir. I'm sorry to disturb you, but you have a call that said it can't wait. Would you like it here or in your office?"

Ross reluctantly let go of Essie's hands and helped her up. "Thank you for an exuberant workout."

"Thanks for joining me. I'll go and get breakfast started. It shouldn't be long. I didn't expect you up this early."

"It's no problem. I never eat before working out. Please take your time." He then turned to Quincy. "Thank you. I'll take it in my office."

As Ross left Essie in the exercise room, he wanted both to curse and thank Quincy for his second, not-so-well-timed, interruption.

Chapter 11

Essie prepared breakfast for Ross and even got to score a few points with Chef Scott by asking him for advice on Ross's preferences, and by helping the chef with prepping the crew's breakfast. She was putting the finishing touches on Ross's tray as Simon gave her a gentle ribbing.

"He won't like it," Simon said, his tone light and teasing as he referred to the fruit kale smoothie she added to the tray.

"You wanna bet?"

Simon looked her up and down, then shook his head. "Nah. The money would be too easy. You do yourself a favor and heat one of your sweet pastries from last night. I know Ross, and no matter how much fruit you try and sweeten it with, he's not drinking that green smoothie."

Essie rolled her eyes and took the tray. "I'll just leave and take that as a compliment on my baking, Chef."

Simon laughed.

As Essie made her way toward Ross's office, she once again almost literally ran into him as he came down the stairs. "Hi. I was just bringing this to you," she said, keeping a tight hold on the tray and her unsteady emotions.

His sudden appearance towering on the stairs surprised her. He was clean and freshly showered in easy sweatpants, which hung low on his hips, and he wore a finely threaded cotton tee, which defined his muscles well. He was no less powerful from when she saw him at the heavy bag that morning, and his clean, freshly showered smell and close presence set her off-kilter. Thankfully, he reached out and took the tray from her hands.

"Come, have you eaten?" he asked.

"I have." She'd grazed from her homemade muesli while prepping, and she had her own shake before heading up, too. Their exuberant workout session made her more famished than normal.

"Well, please still join me while I eat. Chat awhile?"

She studied him for a moment. It wasn't like she really could say no. He'd paid for her time for the duration of this trip. And, honestly, it wasn't like she wanted to say no. "Of course. But don't you have work to do?"

He turned to head up the stairs, but instead of turning left and going toward his office, as she expected, he continued up and went to the large salon. "How about we sit outside? You'll find that it's warmed up. We've had to take a detour, and we'll be making a brief stop along the way at my resort in Bermuda."

Essie looked at him in surprise. "But isn't that way off our course? How long will it delay the trip?"

Ross put the tray on the table nearest the doors to the outer deck and then opened them wide, letting in the fresh air. The view of the open water was stunning. The sun had fully risen and the water glistened a gorgeous crystalline blue through the large windows. "Don't worry, it won't delay us long. And it will give me a chance to show you my resort. You'll get an idea of what I'm planning, with the partnership of these investors." He readied to take a seat, but pulled out a chair and gestured for her to sit first.

Essie came over and, instead of sitting, gave him a small shove into the chair. "I thought on the way to Miami you would get a little relaxation. Seems you found a way to find some extra work."

Almost instinctively, Ross pulled her down onto his lap. The easy snug fit had them both looking at each other with a bit of shock. Ross reached up and brought his finger to her cheek. "I didn't go looking for this work. It came and found me."

Essie knew she should get up, push back, act affronted, something. But sitting on Ross's lap, doing exactly what she was doing in that moment, was the only thing she wanted to do, and right where she was, was the only place she wanted to be.

She took in his dark eyes as he looked at her with a raw, unrestrained desire, the type she had never experienced. "I swear, you make me do the most unprofessional and inappropriate things, Ross Montgomery. When I'm around you, I feel like I'm somehow not my usual self."

Those sexy as hell lips quirked a little at that, and she wanted to kiss him again.

"Is that so bad?" he asked.

Essie thought for a moment. "It sure isn't good. What must you think of me? What must the crew?"

He let out a low, husky growl as he pulled her in close and nuzzled at her neck, sending the most decadent thrill sizzling throughout her body.

"Why are you so worried about what the crew thinks, or

what I think for that matter?" he asked as he leaned back a bit and looked up at her seriously, and maybe a little too deeply. "Why not think about yourself and what you want and feel—do you ever do that?"

Once again he read her and came back with a too-clear summary. She was always caring what others thought and putting their needs before her own. Wasn't it just what she was saying was her downfall and what she had to change most about herself? Essie looked at Ross now and came out with the truth. "No, I usually don't ever do that."

He ran a hand lazily up and down her side, the shivers turning into lazy waves that lulled her into some sort of Ross Montgomery spell.

"Is there any particular reason you don't?"

Suddenly he felt too close to home, and Essie wanted to dodge the subject. She shimmied around and reached for his tray, pulling it toward him while trying to get up. Essie pulled the cover off the plate, and once again Ross pulled a skeptical face. Essie laughed. "Really, again? What were you living on?

Drive-through breakfast specials, too? You really have to change your palate." She hoisted herself up.

"*Aww,* come on now," Ross said as Essie went around to the other side of the table.

"Come on, yourself. Pouting isn't cute on a CEO. For lunch you'll join me in the kitchen. I think a lesson is in order."

Ross surprised her by grinning as he held up his smoothie. "Fine. I welcome joining you in the kitchen. I'll show you where the fryer is and we can dispose of whatever monstrosity made this."

Essie rolled her eyes. "That is incredibly healthy and delicious."

Ross laughed, shaking his head. "Well, I finally found the one thing you can't cook." He sipped at it again and grimaced. "You didn't really cook this, did you? You're pulling one over on me."

"Well, technically, it's not cooked."

Ross cocked his head to the side as he put the smoothie down and dug into his omelet and salmon. "Well, therein lies your problem. Food is meant to be cooked."

Now it was Essie's turn to frown. "Why is that a rule?"

"It's my rule."

"And what? Your rules are somehow law or something?"

He shrugged before taking a long pull of coffee. "Or something."

Essie leaned back, crossing her arms. "You are annoyingly self-assured."

"It's not the first time I've heard that, and you have to know I can't say I take it as an insult."

"I'm not saying I meant it as one." Essie let her gaze wander from him as she looked out at the view. Jayce walked by with an easy wave. It was a glorious day and she suddenly longed to go out.

"I'm glad to hear it. Usually it is not said so kindly."

Essie looked at him once again, and there was a hint of something in his eyes. A certain longing. A hurt. For a moment she couldn't help but wonder if it was a woman bringing that look into his eyes. She wanted to ask, but she knew it wasn't her place. And then he blinked, and as she'd seen him do before, his expression quickly changed and he was cool. Not emotionless, but there was no sign of the brief hint of hurt she had seen. Just the smooth assurance he usually exuded.

"The sun is getting strong. Would you join me for a stroll around the deck? We never took that walk last night."

Essie looked at him and thought of Misha and her ever-so-obvious setup. She wondered if he was in on it, too, and felt her lips twist. What if he was? Would that be so bad? What was the harm in having some fun for a change? She'd earned it, working pretty much nonstop this past year. "Fine, but you'll join me in the kitchen after we go out."

"Of course," he said, getting up and heading for the deck's open doors, confident in the knowledge she'd follow. When she didn't immediately, Ross paused and turned back, putting out his hand. "Please walk with me awhile, Essie?"

Fighting not to overthink, Essie reached out and took Ross's hand in her own, ignoring the smooth, easy fit. "Okay, Ross, show me around. But after that, it's my turn and in my kitchen, and you're my student. So I'm in charge?"

He grinned. "Deal," he said with a mischievous look in his eyes. "How about we seal it with a kiss?"

Essie pushed at him playfully, but followed it by pulling him down until his lips met hers once again. She kissed him until she felt they both needed to jump into the water and cool off. Ross's low moan followed by his erection when she rubbed against him was her clear indication she'd gotten the best of him. She pulled back and looked up into his eyes. "I told you, Ross. You make me do the most improper things."

He smiled. "And once again, I'm so glad for it." But he pulled away from her and took her hand again. "Still, I don't want to rush you. At least not an hour into our first full day together. Besides," he said, taking a breath, "if I don't slow down, I may embarrass myself."

Essie couldn't help the inner smile that showed on the outside with that one. She knew she was good-looking enough and did fine with men. At least no one was kicking her out of bed or turning her down, but no one was openly expressing to her that she made them feel out of control. It was nice, if not surprising, and she couldn't help but wonder if it was some sort of line. She looked at Ross and tried to hide her skepticism.

"Sure. Let's walk. Tell me about your project."

As they walked, Ross told her about the resort he was building. It was an offshoot of his Bermuda resort. But closer to Miami. Essie was amazed at the size and scope of the project and the fact that it sounded like a mini utopia, sort of a *Fantasy Island* for the new set. If he could pull it off, it would be great. Not that she'd see the likes of it. It sounded like "if you have to ask the cost, you can't afford it." Single residences, with private chefs, twenty-four-hour maid and concierge service. All top-notch. No amenity spared and, he'd added, practically no wish, within reason, denied. Essie couldn't help the heat that rushed to her cheeks as her mind wandered to the types of hedonistic fantasies she could explore with Ross in a place like that.

They made their way back toward the main salon area, and Ross and Essie took lounge chairs on deck to relax in the sun awhile. Essie turned to him. "The island sounds fabulous, and like it's a huge undertaking. I can see why you've been under so much stress with that in the works, plus your other holdings in the city. What made you take it on? Your resort in Bermuda is already successful."

Ross's expression got serious for a moment before he spoke. "I don't know. Bermuda is wonderful, but I'm ready to expand. In New York I can always go up, and, believe me, I will. But my father made his mark in resorts, and I know he always wanted to do something like this. Could never do something like this. I'm going to be the Montgomery to make it happen."

Essie frowned. "Have you spoken with your father about it? Is he one of your investors?"

Ross's eyes grew cold. "No. He's given up on that part of the business. Told me I was a fool to do it. I plan to prove him wrong. Once and for all."

Something in Ross's voice let her know she'd gone far enough with the questions for one morning. She gave him a smile. "Well, you'll need your strength to do that. What about we hit the kitchen?" She stood and then reached out a hand to pull him up, but Ross pulled her back down on top of him. Her body hit his with a gentle thump.

"I'd much rather spend time learning more about you, Essie."

His lips were strong and self-assured. There was no tentative pretense in this kiss. Ross pulled her into him, his large hands roaming up her thighs and cupping her behind perfectly as if he had some sort of claim to stake as he rubbed her against his hard body. He coaxed her lips apart and his tongue expertly intertwined with hers, stroking against hers until her body was aflame from her toes on up.

Essie let out a moan when he moved a hand from her behind to the underside of her breast. His thumb teased over her nipple in a circular motion and her most intimate spot went instantly to liquid. “Hell, the things you won’t do to get out of cooperating,” she said, her voice a hoarse whisper as she pushed up against his chest.

Ross chuckled. “I didn’t get this far by playing fair.”

Essie came to her feet, taking gulps of air and smoothing down her hair. She looked down at him with narrowed eyes. “No, I don’t think you did.”

Chapter 12

As they stood at the galley counter, side by side, Ross tried his best to concentrate on what Essie was saying and not just stare at her luscious lips, not to mention her curvy hips. He was ready to break out into a sweat. They had already gotten the shrimp stir fried for the spicy Thai salad they were having for lunch, and now he was chopping, or supposed to be chopping, cucumber. But Essie looked so cute at the stove, her hips giving a little wiggle, which he could almost swear she was unaware of, as she stirred the mixture of shrimp, lime, fish sauce, and onions. At first it seemed like a lot to put together, but he had to admit, she made it seem fun and easy. Essie turned and gave him a smile. Damn those lips. His knife slipped and he nicked his finger. "Ouch!"

"Watch it!" She came running over to check him out, pulling his hurt finger toward her for scrutiny. "You have to pay attention or you're going to get hurt. It's not as simple as it looks."

Ross kept staring at her. "Nothing ever is."

Essie pulled him toward the sink as she simultaneously turned off the stove. She rinsed his cut thumb, then dried it. She pulled the first-aid kit down with a quick, no-nonsense air and bandaged him. "It's nothing much, but you have to be careful." She started to plate their lunch then and, without fanfare, served him at the counter.

Her eyes now held a seriousness that Ross didn't want to accept. He leaned in to kiss her, but she backed up and waved a fork.

"Eat. And enjoy your work. But think about being more careful when you're in my kitchen."

He took a bite, then paused to smile. It was good. Essie gave him a nod of pleasure. "You did well for your first try. You can cook. I don't see why you rely on eating out so much. All I can tell from our short time together is that you go way too fast. You're reckless."

Ross gave her a frown. A look that normally would end most conversations, but still Essie continued.

"Save the look, Ross. I see it. It may have gotten you far in business, but if you're not careful, it could be your downfall."

"I doubt that." He said the words, but something about them still hit him hard.

"Really, then why am I here?" At this, Ross raised his brow and she dropped her fork. "That's bullshit, Ross. And it doesn't look good on you. Be serious with me for once. It was Misha who first called me from the ER. Something got you in there, scared as shit. You have a boat called *Serenity,* but it seems like your life is anything but. Why would you even name your boat *Serenity* if your life is full of chaos?"

Ross swallowed, trying hard to push down the truth he was sailing from as fast as his boat would take him. But he let it out. "It's named after my daughter."

Essie stared. Her eyes wide, her mouth shut. He wished more than anything she'd say something. Anything. Just fill the silence. Right now he didn't want it. The silence was worse than anything. Bringing her on board gave him something do to, something to think about besides the fact that he thought just the other day he might die and would be missing another holiday, maybe his final chance to be with his daughter.

Finally she spoke and said just the wrong thing. "I'm sorry."

"I don't need your pity. I'm fine," Ross said in a low voice.

She laughed and somehow it made him feel better. "Yeah, I can see you are."

Ross laughed then, too. "You really are a ball-buster, you know that?"

Essie surprised him by chuckling. "You know, that's about the nicest thing you could have said to me."

Essie was glad to break the tension. She could see Ross's inner struggle, and though she wanted to be a little hard on him, she felt bad for causing him pain. It was clear that his emotions were erratic and raw. He warred with something in his mind and heart. Essie's own heart broke a little for him and she chided herself for it.

Shit. Now she remembered seeing behind his desk the photo of the little girl. She was so taken with him that she didn't look past the obvious and see deeper. Essie wanted to hang her head in shame. She was so focused on her own desires, she completely shut out what was happening with her client.

Essie could see Ross was uncomfortable, so she eased her way back to his daughter as they shared dessert, a simple brownie a la mode, which he helped make. "How old is your daughter?"

He swallowed before he answered on a low whisper. "She's four."

The answer took her cracked heart and shattered it. One, because of her age, and two, because it seemed to put to rest any buried thought of a blossoming relationship with him.

"I can tell you miss her."

Ross shrugged. "You can't miss what you never had. I was only with Yasmine, Serenity's mother, for the first year of her life. A little less. I never even shared an actual birthday with her. I was on my grind, and I thought Yasmine was all for that, in the beginning. After Serenity, she changed. Said she wanted to settle down, and if it wasn't with me, then it would be with someone she could make a home with. I get it. For some women, they need that." He gave Essie a pointed look.

"Why are you looking at me like that?"

"I'm just looking," he said.

"Well, you're looking like you're sizing me up, which there is no need to, since I'm only here for ten days. Besides, we're talking about you and your daughter."

"Touché." Ross let out a sigh. "No matter, Yas and I were spending more time apart than together. Her modeling career was on a downturn and she was ready to settle down. I was not, and, besides, a kid needs stability. I get it. Her new husband has done well by her and Serenity. We talk and Skype. She knows I'm her father."

Essie wanted to say something, but the way he ended his speech, it made her wonder if he'd be receptive to anything she had to say. She took a gamble. "I'm sure she does and I'm sure, even if you don't think so, she misses you. Especially at Christmas. I know I miss my dad."

Ross's expression had her instantly regretting her words. "It's just he worked a lot. And it was only on his forced time off, Sundays and holidays like Christmas, when we got to spend time together as a family. I cherish that more than I think he ever knew." She smiled as the good times with her dad came back to her. The laughter and the good food they shared. "It was my father who first taught me how to cook."

Ross's eye widened. "Was he a chef, too?"

She shook her head. "Oh, no! Just a hungry man with a creative palate. Dad never made the same dish twice. It was always a little different, depending on what we had available. His only day off from driving the bus was Sunday, and he loved cooking for my mother. She worked so hard, so he'd make her these wonderful meals with whatever we had on hand. As I got a little bigger, I'd join him in the kitchen, and we'd laugh together and he'd tell me stories of his family, how one day it would be great to have a family restaurant where we could do this all the time. In the kitchen was the only place he wasn't stressed about bills, time, the next shift."

Ross glided the back of his hand softly and reassuringly along her arm. She gave him a smile as she continued speaking. "He always said we were blessed that God made a way so that we always had a little food on the table. My father died on a Sunday, going in to make a little overtime to get more for our holiday dinner. Christmas was our favorite time. Trimming the tree. Sharing a meal." Essie stopped talking when Ross reached out and wiped a tear from her cheek, which she hadn't known she'd shed. "Oh, hell. I'm sorry," she said.

"What are you sorry for? It's me who should be apologizing. Taking you away from your mother on Christmas. No job or amount of money is worth that."

She put her hand out to his lips to stop him. "No, this was my choice. You're bringing me closer to my dream of my own restaurant, and I thank you." She smiled wide, hoping to elevate the mood. "Now, enough talk. Let me clean this up, and you take care of whatever you planned for this afternoon, and I'll think up your next fabulous meal."

Chapter 13

As *Serenity* docked in Bermuda, Essie didn't know what to expect. Ross told her his business for his resort wouldn't be more than a couple of hours. It was some trouble with the contractor who was doing renovations on his new state of the art golf course. But still, Ross planned on spending the day there. He wanted to take her out, to show her around, and then they could have dinner together before boarding and heading out to continue their trip to Miami.

She had to admit she was excited, but also hesitant. Ross wasn't the type of guy she was used to dating. And it wasn't as if they were even dating. As soon as they got off the boat, Essie spied the two drivers, with matching Mercedes sedans, waiting for them and knew this wouldn't be her usual roughing-it trek. *What? No mopeds available?*

Ross kissed her easily, as if they were a couple in a comfortable, much longer relationship, when, in reality, they were anything but. She couldn't help but marvel at his outward show of confidence. Though when they were alone and talking, without the buffer of a sexual flame, she picked up on definite insecurities that waved off him. But Ross did an excellent job of not letting it show. Regarding the crew, he felt no need to make any explanations or excuses about their heating relationship; and, in turn, he encouraged her not to feel it necessary to do so, either. His strong confidence left no room for any second-guessing, and she found she barely got a second glance when she went in to make breakfast this morning.

Part of it bugged her. Made it feel like them hooking up was something the crew knew was inevitable from the moment she stepped on the ship. It also made her wonder how often he did such a thing.

As Ross pulled back from their kiss, he stared at Essie hard. "You're overthinking," he said.

She frowned. "You're right, I am. And it's a waste of time on such a beautiful day." Essie gave him a smile and rose up to kiss him, this time enjoying the thrill of his lips against hers. When would she get this opportunity again?

When she pulled away, he was smiling down at her. "I got you your own car for the afternoon. You take it into town, do some shopping." He reached into his pocket and pulled out some bills.

Essie shook her head. "I'll take the car, but I draw the line at taking your money."

Ross sighed. "There's my favorite judge. I was wondering where she went. How about doing your job? Do you mind buying some more fresh produce for the boat?"

Essie looked down, feeling bad for not giving him the benefit of the doubt. "Sorry," she said, her voice low as she took the bills.

"Never be." He kissed her as he moved around the driver and opened the door for her to get in the car. He kissed her once more. "You're too sweet to be sorry. Have the driver bring you by the resort around four. I'll show you around, and we'll have dinner."

As he closed the door and headed toward his own waiting car, Essie fought hard against her sudden feelings of missing him.

She had the driver drop her off at a spot in town, giving him no further direction except to make it as touristy as possible. She only had a few hours, so she might as well do it up. *Candy-colored houses and Bermuda shorts, bring it on!*

Essie explored the cobblestone lanes and colorful facades. She tried to get into the quaint cobblestone streets and the pretty shops, but the high number of couples—hand in hand, and arm in arm—kept bringing her thoughts annoyingly back to Ross. And she knew that thinking of him, or anyone for that matter, right now in the realm of couple's vacations, matching outfits, and long walks, was a total waste of mental energy.

Essie paused outside a pretty local art shop window, where there was a display of necklaces. It was funny how she didn't miss Cam at all. At least not in the way she thought she would. And here she was, just a week ago as he was walking out her door, thinking she'd miss him for a long time to come. Showed what a waste the past two years with him had been.

A lovely blue stone necklace caught her eye and made her think of her mom. No use mooning over any of this, but she'd get something for her mother. She'd already gotten her the pretty scarf she'd wanted, but this would be a bonus to make up for being away. That decided, Essie walked into the shop.

As Essie left the shop, her mom's gift in hand, she went in

search of her car and driver, having decided she was set on having him take her to shop for fresh local food. Doing the tourist thing was a bore. She'd have more fun searching for ingredients.

Once they arrived at the roadside stalls, Essie was in heaven. So many fresh fruits and vegetables, not to mention fish. She knew that before going to the resort to meet Ross, they'd have to pick up a cooler or head back to the boat so the food wouldn't spoil.

At one stall Essie was so engrossed in conversing with a local woman about the tripe stew she was making, she didn't notice the tall man getting close to her until he was almost upon her.

"You like it spicy?" he asked, his leering tone letting her know he definitely wasn't asking about the stew.

Essie looked around for her driver, but saw he wasn't by the car. *Shit.* She pointedly ignored the man and paid the woman for two take-out bowls of her stew. As she tried to walk away and head across the road to the car, the man followed close. Too close.

"I asked you a question."

Essie kept walking until his hand came out and he made a move to turn her back in his direction.

"What? You too fancy to answer me, miss—"

Almost simultaneously a dark figure came into Essie's field of vision, and she saw Mr. Handsy crumble to the ground. He howled as his hands clutched his bleeding nose.

"I'm sorry it took me so long to get here."

Essie looked up, her wide eyes meeting Ross's own. "But I was supposed to be meeting you."

He shrugged, unfazed by the man now on the ground, clutching his bleeding nose, and the gathering crowd. "And I'm here to meet you. I'm still sorry I took so long. You shouldn't have had to deal with the likes of him."

"What the hell, man?" Mr. Spicy said while attempting to right himself.

Ross looked down at the man. He had such a hard glint in his eyes, it almost made Essie back up. He stepped on the man's outstretched fingers, causing him to writhe in pain. "Get up. I dare you. You need to watch who and whose you make a move on next time." He reached into his pocket and pulled out a bill and dropped it on the man's chest. "Consider yourself lucky I'm feeling so good right now. Go get yourself cleaned up and something to eat." He took Essie by the hand and led her to the waiting car. It was then that she noticed the cars had been switched. Her driver was gone and it was his car and driver.

"Where has my driver gone?" Essie asked as she got inside.

"Back to the dock. He's taken your other packages back to *Serenity*. Take us to the resort, please," Ross said. The last bit was meant for their driver before Ross hit a switch and the partition between them and the driver rose.

The look Ross gave Essie was one of pure primal sex and energy; it had the next question dying on her lips, forgotten instantly. He reached for her, and instead of putting her hand in his, she was on him. On top and straddling and kissing him, hard and fast and wet. She wore an easy sundress, which let her thighs go wide, and left her deliciously exposed and open to him. She rubbed urgently against his hard erection, her feminine center feeling like it was on fire. And for the first time in her life, Essie wanted to strip off her clothes and see what it felt like to be taken hard and fast by a man she barely knew.

The feeling made her not recognize herself, and she felt slightly afraid of the person Ross was unleashing. She moved from his lips to lick at the side of his neck. Wanting to go further, with shaky hands, she undid the buttons on his shirt and was rewarded by the sight of his hard chest and dark nipples. Essie leaned down and nipped at the beautiful tight nubs.

Ross groaned and grabbed her thighs, pushing forward. His hardness and the zipper of his pants were roughly rubbing against her. One of his large hands moved to her breasts, and Essie moved back, pulling the straps of her dress down, along with her bra. It wasn't elegant, and it wasn't beautiful, but she didn't care. He was elegant, and he was beautiful, and slightly rough, and aggressive, and she wanted him on her, in her, wherever, however, she could have him.

Thankfully, he obliged, drawing one of her nipples almost reverently into his mouth and licking it as if it were the most delicate of desserts. She felt him pulse beneath her, and breathed in deep as his hand went up her thigh and almost shakily reached under her dress to clutch at her behind. She could tell he was doing his best to hold on to his hairsbreadth of control.

"Why are you holding back, Ross?" she choked out, almost wanting to shake him as she saw his Adam's apple bob.

He looked up, a bead of sweat popping out on his forehead as he put his head back. "Because I don't want to let go with you. I don't want to just take you in the back of one of my cars."

Essie swallowed, torn between telling him taking her in the back of one of his cars was just what she wanted, and knowing it definitely wasn't. She leaned down and kissed him gently. "Then take me to your bed, Ross Montgomery."

Ross set Essie to rights as they pulled onto his resort's grounds. She rolled down the window to catch her breath and take in the scenery—lush green and well-manicured grounds. They drove past a beautiful yellow main house that looked like it had maybe a hundred rooms, and off to the side of the main house were smaller villas. Around them were private balconies, and little golf carts sprinkled here and there.

Their car kept going, and when Ross caught her questioning look, he gave her a small smile. "We're going right to my private villa. I thought it best we dine alone. I hope that's all right."

Essie blushed. "It's fine, but maybe we should eat and then head back to the boat. I don't want you to get off schedule."

Ross leaned in close. "We can do whatever you want. I will work around you. If you want to stay here tonight, we stay here. If you want to go, we go."

Essie looked at him as the car stopped. "I'd like to see your place here."

Ross's villa was so very him: minimalist, elegant, and sexy. Open concept with a large sitting area for entertaining and two bedrooms off to the side. The back of the villa was all floor-to-ceiling windows, which opened to a spectacular view of the fabled pink sand beach and had Essie gasping for breath. Out on the veranda, dinner was set with fresh seafood, sweets, champagne, and desserts.

"Ross, it's gorgeous. I don't think I've ever seen a beach so beautiful and all this food. We didn't need my stew after all." He came up behind her at the window and kissed the back of her neck, giving her a thrill that vibrated throughout her entire body.

"I think so, too. When I'm here, I can relax. Or, at least, my version of relaxing."

Essie laughed at that.

"That part of the beach is mine and private. When we have more time, I'd love to bring you back here to swim with me."

At his declaration she couldn't help but feel a little sad.

"What is it?" he asked.

"That. You don't have to make any sort of promise of anything beyond this trip. I know you can't. That's okay. Let's enjoy *now.*"

Ross's lips twisted, but he didn't argue with her. "Don't look so sad. CEOs don't do sad." She moved forward to kiss him. "Now I think there are more parts of this villa you can show me. I'd love to see the master suite. That is, if dinner will wait?"

At that, Ross picked her up and threw her over his shoulder. He gave her a light smack on her behind. "Oh, hell yeah, dinner will wait. If I have my way, it will wait until breakfast."

"Hey, I don't think this is the standard tour!" Essie kicked and giggled.

He laughed, low and deep in his throat. "It's the way I do a tour. We're not in the backseat anymore, Ms. Bradford."

Chapter 14

Despite the rough way he picked her up, Ross gently placed her down crossways on his large bed. He then pulled back, going to his knees to take off her slip-on shoes. He came up and kissed her long and hard, leaving her almost gasping for breath, before he eased up, to start a sweet, almost torturous, trail down her body.

Essie thought he'd linger on her collarbone, her breasts maybe, which he teased with his thumb through her dress, but no. He skimmed those spots, going lower, down to her ankles, spending time kissing them, making an anklet of feathery kisses, then working his way until he was behind her knee. When he got a desired response from her, he'd lick and nibble some more. As he was licking behind her knee, and she was distracted by the newfound glory of that particular erogenous zone, Ross's hand worked its way up to her most private spot, and he pulled her panties down as he brought his head higher.

With his first lick Essie thought she'd break apart. She was biting her lip and balling her fists tight so as not to come completely undone.

Ross was masterful. He licked and she rocked. He sucked and she rode. She was clenching and unclenching her hands until she grasped at his shoulders, letting go as she never had before. And when she finally reached her peak, with his name echoing as breathy gasps on her lips, Ross pulled back, tugging her dress over her head, taking her bra off, and giving her breast a last, long, gentle kiss.

"God, Essie, you are gorgeous," he rasped out.

Her instinct was to cover up, as gooseflesh suddenly tickled over her body. But something in his hot, admiring gaze made her feel so incredibly beautiful, she could do no more but reach for him. Essie kissed Ross hard and passionately. Undoing his shirt and pulling it out of his pants.

"You have on way too many clothes, Mr. Montgomery."

"You are so right there," he said, breathing heavy.

As she freed him, Ross handed her a condom. Essie sucked in an anxious breath. He was glorious. But her awkwardness came out in her ineptitude with slipping on the condom, and she was thankful for Ross's help. His hand steadied hers as he guided her in easing it down over his hardness.

His first thrust stole her breath away with its power; and when she came once again, looking into the depths of his midnight eyes, he kissed her, sealing their moment with an unspoken promise of the next week of more glorious lovemaking to come.

They spent the next few hours making love in every way and every place in his villa, the bed, the Jacuzzi, his large shower. Somewhere in between, dinner got eaten, and Ross even convinced Essie to take a mad naked dash from his villa to the beach and into the water. Or maybe it was the other way around. Essie laughed so much she couldn't remember when she'd last enjoyed such a night. In fact, she knew she hadn't.

Just before dawn she woke with Ross kissing her shoulder. "I'm sorry to wake you so early, but do you mind if we get going to the boat? The captain may have to push it to make it to Miami in time with the delay."

Essie could feel his tension and didn't want him to stress. She turned and kissed him lightly. "It's fine. Just give me a minute to get ready." She stroked at his hardness playfully. "And stop being so serious. Just because we're back on the boat and I'll have you back to your routine, you'll still have me in your bed. There's no way I'm giving this up before New York."

Ross grinned and nipped at her shoulder again. "Whew. That's a relief."

❄ ❄ ❄

When they arrived back on *Serenity,* Essie was shocked.

The boat, which had been decorated luxuriously, was now decked out for Christmas with lovely twinkling lights and sprigs of holly and evergreen. And there in the main parlor was a large undecorated Christmas tree. She turned to Ross with shimmering tears she wasn't capable of hiding. "Ross, it's beautiful, but why? How?"

"I couldn't let you not have Christmas," he said in a matter-of-fact way. "I thought while I was handling the contractor, I'd have the boys pick up a tree, festive the old girl up a bit. I had them save the tree decorating for you though."

Essie grinned then looked at him with barely restrained hope. "Will you do it with me?"

Ross made a face. "It's not my thing."

Essie's smile widened. "Well, let's make it your thing. We'll do it together. After dinner. Please. Decorating a Christmas tree is always better with friends. We'll invite the crew."

Ross shook his head, but something in his eyes lit. "Sure. Anything for that smile."

❄ ❄ ❄

Dinner was casual and shared with the crew, once they got under way again. Essie and Chef Scott collaborated on the meal. She was glad they had come to a mutual working relationship, though he was still a bit gruff around the edges. They casually dined on shrimp rolls, haddock, and spicy noodles, since Essie had quickly learned that Ross loved all things with either a touch of sweet or plenty of spice. Plus, a lovely blend of mixed vegetables. There was wine for everyone, and the captain joined them while Ethan took over his duties for a while on the bridge.

When Essie came in with dessert, homemade ice cream with dark chocolate mulled wine sauce, the captain stood and raised his glass in a toast. "To Ms. Bradford. Thank you for gracing us with your beauty and your talent. You are making this maiden voyage a sweet excursion."

Ross grinned and stood, coming over to kiss Essie lightly on her cheek. But the crew would not be satisfied with that, and they cheerfully started to clink on their wineglasses with their tableware. "Kiss! Kiss!"

Essie gave them a wave of her hand. "You all are incorrigible! Thank you so much. You almost make me not miss New York and the holiday snow. Almost."

But they would not be mollified. When Ross clinked his glass, too, she relented, taking Ross's cheeks in both hands. For a moment she enjoyed the feel of his scruff and pulled him in for a big, sloppy kiss. The guys all cheered as she pulled back.

"Okay, enough with you all. Bring your desserts around the tree. Let's get Christmas started!"

They all took turns adding the pretty gold and silver ornaments. The captain left early, letting Ethan come to take his place. When it was done and the rest of the crew left, Essie sat on the low couch as Ross turned down the lights and flipped the switch on the tree.

"It's lovely," she said as he put his arm around her and nuzzled her in close, kissing her behind her ear.

"Why is it I feel there's a 'but' in there?" Ross asked.

"There is no 'but.' It is lovely. It's just so elegant—more elegant than any tree I've ever had. Ours at home is jam-packed with mismatched ornaments. My mom made a point of buying or we made a new one every year. Maybe it's something you could do with your daughter?"

But at the mention of the child, she saw Ross's eyes go dark and cloud over. She knew instantly she'd made a mistake. Trying hard to bring the moment back, Essie spoke rapidly to cover the awkward moment. "My mom still buys me one, and I'm no spring chicken."

Ross pulled back then quickly leaned forward, nipping at her lips teasingly. "Get out! You can't be a day past twenty-two."

Essie laughed as she rolled her eyes, glad to be back on sure footing. It was fun to sit with him and be playful for a while. "I won't tell you how many years to add to that. But thanks again. I really do appreciate it. I know you weren't into the holiday. I just think it should be shared with family and those you love. But this"—Essie paused—"this is really nice. But I didn't mean to force it on you."

He looked at her and ran a hand up and down her thigh. "You didn't. No one forces anything on me."

Essie snorted. "Now, that I believe!"

"I wanted to make you happy. With you missing your holiday with your mom," he laughed then, "and the cold New York snow and all. You can't really be missing that."

She looked at him seriously. "I sure am. Who doesn't dream of a white Christmas? You can't be hardened to that. What's Christmas without snow?"

Ross shook his head. "You really are a sweet traditionalist, Essie Bradford. I don't know what you're doing here in my arms. A man like me would ruin you."

His last words were low and serious, and something about them made Essie's heart stop for a moment with a deep fear of loss she knew she had no right to have.

"What are you talking about?"

"Nothing," he said too quickly. "I guess I'm not used to any downtime. See what you did to me? Went and got me thinking." He pulled her tighter to him. "And you got me thinking about things with my daughter, too. I don't know." He looked down then and let out a sigh. "I guess things need to change."

She leaned in and kissed him. She didn't want to see him sad, and she didn't want to make this moment heavy. Soon enough they'd make it to Miami and before too long her assignment would be over.

Their kiss changed quickly from sweet to deep and passionate; and before long, Essie was breaking apart again, beside herself and feeling out of herself, all at the same time. She took a deep breath and then pushed up from Ross and the couch. She looked into his passion-darkened eyes and took him by the hand. "Your stateroom or mine?"

He stood. Tall and powerful, towering over her. "I'll let you choose. I always want this to be your choice. Your terms, Essie."

She smiled. "Yours, then. I want to try out all the beds you can offer me while on the trip, Mr. Montgomery."

He grinned and gave a quick nod. "Then let's go. What's mine is yours, Ms. Bradford."

❄ ❄ ❄

When *Serenity* pulled into Miami's Biscayne Bay, Essie steeled herself against her heavy heart. She and Ross had spent a blissful three days together on board, both in bed and out. Their days were unstructured and carefree, and their nights were spent making love in ways she'd only fantasized about.

She cooked for him, and he surprised her by spending quite a bit of time with her in the kitchen, learning what she hoped were lasting lessons about food choices and the benefits of cooking for himself. They also had a lot of fun in the gym, with her giving him the benefits of yoga and meditation, and him giving her the basics of kickboxing. More times than not, their sparring ending up with either Essie or Ross flat on their back, one pinned under the other.

This time spent with him would go down as some of the best days of her life—at least the most fun and carefree. And reluctantly, when she felt him standing strong by her side, his arm draped easily over her shoulder, rubbing her arm in that endearing, absentminded way he'd taken to doing, she had to admit she was going to miss this. No, she was going to miss *him,* when all was said and done. A knot twisted in Essie's belly as the butterflies seemed to bunch up in one corner.

Shit. I'm falling for him.

But as Essie saw the stretch limo waiting for them as they departed, flanked by a female driver and two other beautiful women in short skirts and tight blazers, she couldn't help but stiffen. Normally, she was more confident. Seeing these women, who looked like versions of every woman she'd seen pictured with him, something in her deflated. It brought to mind the fact that it would all be over in days. But Essie forced herself to shake it off as a tall, slim young man stepped forward and came up to them.

"Good to see you, sir," he said before sparing Essie a glance. "And good to see you, too, Ms. Bradford."

Though Essie didn't know him, he did know her, and he seemed unsurprised by the intimacy of her and Ross's entwined hands. It raked at her and she stiffened.

"Essie, this is my assistant, Andrew Vaughn."

Essie gave the younger man a nod. "Nice to meet you, Mr. Vaughn." She let go of Ross and stuck out her hand.

"You too. I hope your trip went well. Please let me know of any supplies you need for the return, and I'll be sure to have them brought on board."

"Thank you. I think I'm pretty good. I do prefer to do my

own shopping, but I'd appreciate it if you know Miami or have someone else who does, that could point me in the direction of the freshest markets."

Andrew nodded.

"Is everything all set and ready?" Ross asked.

"Yes, sir. You'll see these are the types of cars and drivers with the ladies as concierge that we sent to pick up the clients. They should be arriving at *Serenity* within the next two hours."

Essie was intently following along. It was a good thing Andrew was explaining because he wasn't giving out any introductions to the ladies. Essie thought of introducing herself but the women gave off a sort of aloofness that could tag the part of a gorgeous female spy ring or darned good exclusive club bouncers. A small bus pulled up and two more beautiful women got out, along with two men who were just as model gorgeous. They lined up next to Andrew. "These are Lacey, Ana, Marco, and Louis. Additional staff for guest-stew services."

Essie didn't miss the hot look Lacey gave Ross. It was an invite, an openness, as Andrew continued his introductions.

"They will be available for the clients for any and all entertainment while on board. Marco and Louis will help with deckhand services and anything else that is needed."

Essie couldn't help but bristle. *Serenity* was about to become quite the party ship, and she couldn't help but wonder at what type of services and or entertainment Andrew was referring to. But Essie pushed the thoughts back. She and Chef Scott would have plenty of mouths to feed. Playtime, at least for her, was definitely over. Though Chef Scott was a jerk, she would pitch in and help him with so many passengers coming aboard.

"Well," she said, looking up at Ross, "I guess I'd better get going with supplies so I can get back to help out Simon. We're about to get really busy."

Ross bent and gave her a kiss. "Fine, but Simon can handle the bulk of the cooking. You take this car and get what you want him to prepare. I want you by my side tonight. I'll stay here with Andrew, making a few calls if you don't mind."

Ross's words about being by his side pulled her up short, but Essie tried not to make too much of them. "Not at all."

But as Ross pulled away, he gave her a long stare. "Don't worry, I'll watch out. No buying stew in dodgy neighborhoods. And I won't be long. I want to be back"—she looked over the leggy woman eyeing Ross like the last crab leg at the all-you-can-eat buffet—"before things get too wild."

Chapter 15

Essie made it back on board *Serenity* at the same time as the clients—a ruckus crew of three couples. Two married—the Cruzes and the Johnsons—and the other, an owner of a basketball team, Jimmy Paul, and his girlfriend, a model named Lola.

Essie tugged on her top and smoothed her disheveled hair as she was introduced to the bejeweled women. She didn't mean to be late, but while out shopping for supplies, she ran across the sweetest little Christmas shop. Though rushed, she couldn't help but go in. Once there she picked up an ornament for her mom. Though this one would be late, her mom would still love it. And when she saw they personalized ornaments, Essie couldn't resist getting a beautiful one with snowmen and palm trees, which she had personalized with the name Serenity. She hoped Ross would use it to both remember her, and to start a new tradition with his daughter when he was ready.

After the awkward introductions, Essie left the gift on her dresser and quickly changed for dinner, which as it turned out would be off board at a Miami hot spot.

Later, sitting on the deck with Mrs. Cruz, who refused an individual tart, as well, Essie noticed, as most of her dinner, Essie made attempts at small talk. There had to be a reason Ross wanted her here. Maybe playing hostess was it. "Though I'm sure you enjoy Miami, tell me, are you looking forward to traveling back to New York?" Essie asked. The woman was silent and had been for the past ten minutes. It was like pulling teeth, getting a word out of her.

"Surprising," Mrs. Cruz said as she turned and examined her with a critical eye.

"Excuse me?"

"It's you. You're surprising." She looked over at one of the new stews, the pretty Ana, who was serving a drink to Mr. Cruz in the Jacuzzi while showing off her cleavage to its best advantage. "Now that's more his usual."

The cutting comment from the woman hit Essie at her core and she felt heat rise in her cheeks. Her instincts were to argue. She had her talents and it was a waste to let insecurities over legs and boobs fill sacred space in her spirit. She was the one that Ross asked to be here. Well, technically, paid to be here. Just like every other female on this ship. Essie let out a low breath as she spotted Ana handing Ross a drink and adding an extra touch to his bared bicep with it. Her argument died in her throat.

Essie tried to shake off her sudden unwelcome uneasiness when Ross turned and gave her a smile that was more head than heart. The tranquil peace of The Serenity was gone. And as Essie lay down that night cradled in Ross's arms, spent from making love, the waves gently rocking the boat, she didn't sleep soundly.

❄ ❄ ❄

It was morning and they were now under way to head to Ross's private island, where the resort would be built. It was a short boat ride away, just four hours. Near enough to Miami for party shuttles to go, and far enough for him to create his own secluded oasis.

The butterflies that had befriended her started up again, but this time their fluttering brought the most unwelcome feeling. She was not looking forward to her time with this bunch. And though she'd tried her best to straddle the line of help and hostess, Essie had not received a kind look or gesture since she met any of them. She feared the time back to New York with them would not go well.

As if feeling Essie's unease, Ross turned her way and gave her a warm smile. The butterflies eased down and she smiled back. She was probably being nutty and should just chill. Essie relaxed and decided to ignore the pinched faced women and enjoy herself, as she had been.

But things didn't get better on the island. Though the tour was fascinating, and Essie could totally see Ross's exciting vision, she was once again pulled up short by their arrival to the fanfare of scantily clad women and a few men scattered within. Drinks flowed like water and the promise of all the hedonism imaginable was thick in the air. Essie's unease grew as she watched Ross seem to swell bigger, louder, and bolder, until he somehow was wearing a mask of himself that no longer fit. But maybe this was him and the Ross she got to know when it was just the two of them was a mask he was wearing to woo her into his bed? The thought stopped her short.

By the time the tour was over, and their party on board *Serenity* readying to head back to Miami, the party had swelled to one with a band and dancing girls, two to each man, in Ross's case three, as the women seemed to want to be sure their check writer knew exactly who they were. And Ross played it up, sharing cigars all around while being loud and boisterous.

When Ross, at the encouragement of the crowd, took a shot from between the breasts of a curvy brunette in a barely there bikini and turned to Essie suggesting she do the same, she was done. She had a splitting headache and wanted to retreat and go to bed, away from this version of Ross.

"Come on, babe, go for it! This is a party. Why don't you act like it?"

Essie eyed the way Ross's hands were grasping the hips of the brunette and wanted to step out of the whole scene. She looked into his slightly unfocused eyes and felt both anger and sadness. Anger for being put in this situation and sadness over what she'd hoped it would be. "This is not my type of party Ross. And I'm tired."

Ross frowned and looked ready to argue, but Essie got her opening when Mrs. Johnson dropped her makeshift toga and shimmied naked to get under the limbo pole more easily. The crowd cheered and Essie got up and started heading across the room. But Ross saw her heading toward the stairs, and before she knew it, he was there at her side.

"Where you going?"

"Like I said, I'm tired, Ross. I think I'll leave you to your clients. It's late and the band is getting to me. I have a headache."

He leaned in to kiss her and his rum-and-cigar breath had her recoiling.

Ross frowned, his darkening eyes surprising her, but not more than the possessive hand on her arm. "But I want you here with me. Besides, I didn't say you were off the clock yet."

Essie heated so fast she felt like she may cause the whole ship to burst into flames. "Screw you, Ross Montgomery. I'm freelance, so I work for myself. You may own everything and everyone else on this boat, but you don't own me."

Ross looked down at his empty hand and closed it into a tight fist. It was all he could do, since all he felt was alone. His first instinct was to go after her. Go after her and pull her back into his arms. Kiss her long and hard with everything he had and let her know how much she meant to him. How he shouldn't have said what he said.

Ross took a step, then stopped short. But what did she mean to him? Did he even know? They'd made no promises to each other, which was probably a good thing. Sure, they had a good time aboard the ship. Secure in the world of just the two of them, but with just this simple test he could see they were no match for the outside world. He thought he had known with Yasmine. Thought he could play the role of happy-home husband and father, but what did he do? He went and fucked that up in less than a year. And now his ex was married to someone else and, worse, his daughter was being raised by another man. He didn't want to relive that all over again with Essie. It had already been proven he was his father's son, and the business was his first and one true love.

But still Essie called to him. If only so he could at least apologize for speaking to her and treating her so harshly. Ross took a step forward and a hand grazed him lightly on his shoulder. He turned to look into the smiling eyes and glossy lips of—what was her name? Lacey?

"Mr. Montgomery, Mr. Paul sent me to retrieve you for a game of Twister. We're all playing and he said I'm not to take no for an answer."

As she said those words, the new steward slipped her polo over her head to reveal a white bikini top. Ross frowned and shook his head. "Please tell Mr. Paul I won't be playing, but to enjoy the game with my compliments."

She put on what Ross thought was a well-practiced pout. "I'm afraid he won't be happy, sir."

Ross suddenly wanted to be anywhere but there. Here he was with everything he thought he wanted: money, women, prestige, and the one thing he really needed was just out of reach. "Tell Mr. Paul to have an enjoyable evening on me," he said before he turned and headed for the stairs.

As Essie slammed the door, hot tears burned at her eyes. *Shit. Why did I ever get so close?* If she hadn't gotten close, he wouldn't have affected her. And what was with that Lacey? She didn't miss her lurking as she waited for her moment—all hair, lips, and boobs at the ready.

Still, Essie took a few deep breaths to calm her nerves. She really was tired, and then she thought for a moment of how tired he must be. He'd been tap-dancing for these people all day, trying to get their backing and support, and still he had more dancing to do. Essie's heart broke a moment for him, and then she saw her bag from the Christmas shop earlier in the day.

She took the ornament out and crossed the hall to leave it on Ross's pillow. A peace offering of sorts to let him know though she was angry, she still cared. Besides, no matter what happened, his daughter should still have the ornament.

Essie woke feeling refreshed and hopeful that she and Ross could get back on track. She dressed to go to the galley, and found Chef Scott was up, already preparing a big breakfast. They were docked in Miami and would be there for a few hours before sailing back to New York with the clients to conclude the deal.

She thought of Ross and their argument the night before and how tired he must be today. But today was a new day and she was ready to start over again. Essie reached into the fridge and took out the last tiny chocolate mousse. "I'm going to take this to Ross. I'll be back in a moment to help you finish up," she said to Simon.

"He's not here."

Essie stilled. "What do you mean?"

"He's gone. Said he had urgent business and left instructions with the captain about returning the passengers to New York without him."

Without him? What was she even hearing? Essie was so confused. Where did he go, and why did he say nothing to her? She went back to her room in a daze and saw a gift bag on her bureau. One she didn't see before. Essie picked it up and numbly went to her bed to open it. Pulling out the mass of tissue paper, Essie didn't see the letter that fell between the bed and her nightstand. But she was surprised to find a snow globe inside with a scene of Miami Beach that when shaken would be covered with snow. Attached was a plane ticket dated today with a Post-it and just the words:

Go home, Ms. Bradford, and get your New York snow.
Thank you for a job well done.

Stay Sweet,
R.M.

Taped to the bottom was Essie's check with her full fee, plus her agreed-upon ten-thousand-dollar bonus. As Essie packed, she silently cursed her stupid tears. This was only supposed to be a little bit of fun, she told herself. Something to get over the hump so to speak. It was her own fault, opening her heart to a man who was only hiring her for a quick fix, nothing more. She'd done her job and now it was over. That should be enough. But as Essie walked the gangplank and left The Serenity behind, she couldn't help feeling completely undone.

❄ ❄ ❄

It was indeed snowing, and had been since Essie returned home. She'd received one text from Ross asking if she made it home safely. She guessed that as far as employers went, he didn't have to do that much. She replied to him with just two words I did.

They had no further communication.

It was now New Year's Eve and she was with her mom at her apartment. They were sharing a meal of good-luck peas and rice, waiting for the ball to drop on TV. She was sure by 12:15 a.m. it would be lights out. Way to start the New Year. *Woo to the freaking hoo.*

So when the doorbell rang at 11:30 p.m., they both looked at each other, wide-eyed, New York instincts going on full alert.

Essie went to the door. "Who is it?" she yelled with extra bass in her voice before looking out the peephole.

"It's me, Essie."

She knew the voice, but didn't believe her ears, so she took a look through the peephole. *Damn.* It was him. Tall, magnetic, his dark eyes seemed to connect with hers through the peephole, and then he had the nerve to have that smile. How did he even know she'd be here tonight? This had Misha written all over it. She'd kill her.

"What are you doing here?" Essie yelled.

"I'm here to see you. You going to open the door, or does the whole floor have to know your business? I'm fine either way."

Hesitantly, Essie opened the door a crack before finally gesturing for him to come in. No use letting the neighbors know her business. Her mom stood and looked at him with a strong and well-deserved side eye. "This is my mother."

Ross reached out a hand. "It's nice to meet you, Mrs. Bradford. I've heard wonderful things about you."

Her mom gave him a hard eye. "Can't say the same about you."

Ross looked confused as Essie crossed her arms. "If you're here to hire me for another job, the answer is no."

"What are you talking about?"

"What do you mean, what am I talking about? You leave without a word? Just a ticket? You turned out to be the rich jerk I pegged you for in the beginning. Judgy? Me? Hell yeah!"

"You didn't get my letter with the ticket?"

"What, your Post-it? Classy rich boy."

"Post-it?" He furrowed his brow; then recognition and then a bit of horror dawned in his eyes. His words came fast and desperate. "No. My letter. I enclosed a letter and told you I was so sorry for the night before. I didn't want to deal with those clients anymore, and I didn't want you to, either. I told you that you were right. That the holidays should be spent with the people you love the most. With family. So I went to see my daughter. I wanted to give her the ornament you gave me. And I wanted you to be with your mom at Christmas."

There was a sharp "oh" as Essie's mom took in Ross's speech. Ross grinned as Essie's mother made a polite exit to the other room. His smile widened when he turned and took in Essie's stunned expression and slack jaw.

Ross walked over to her and cautiously wrapped her in his arms. The chill of the outside still on his coat gave her a delicious shiver as he opened it and she eased into the warmth of his chest.

She looked up at him. "I can't believe you did that for me."

"Woman, neither can I. But I'm coming to find out there's not much I wouldn't do for you. So here I am. I'm so sorry for what I put you through. For how I treated you and spoke to you. It was uncalled for and will *never* happen again. I was showing off, drinking too much, and being all around just too much. Just like I wrote in the letter, which you obviously didn't get, I was an ass that night and I apologize. In my short time with you, you opened my eyes so much. You let me know what is truly important in life, and spending the holiday on a boat, named after the person I love dearly, with people I don't care about, well, there was just something wrong with that. And when you walked away from me that night, I knew I had to make it right."

His words stunned Essie. She was stunned by his openness and trust in her with sharing so much of himself.

Ross kissed her softly on her temple and continued. "I hope I can make it right with you. Because here I am taking off work on another holiday in order to spend it with the only other woman besides my daughter that I can say I love."

Essie froze.

Now it was her turn to gasp out a shocked "oh!" But when Ross's lips came down on hers, and New York exploded as the crystal ball dropped and midnight struck, New Year's Day began for the both of them with the promise of a lifetime of sweet serenity.

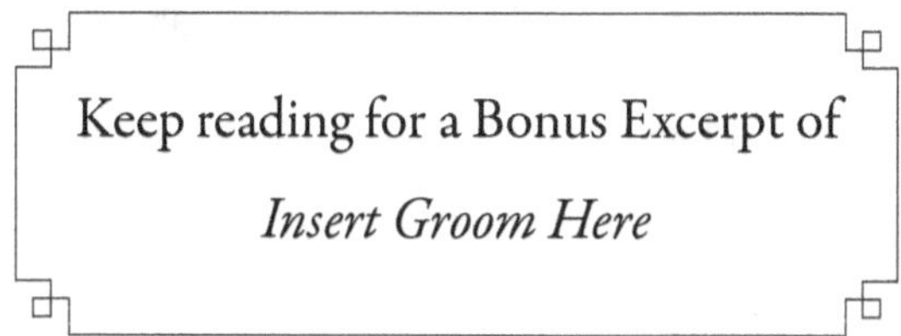

BONUS EXCERPT

Insert Groom Here

Chapter 1

"*I can't marry you.*"

Eva Ward knew words were being murmured over her shoulder, but for the life of her she couldn't quite make them out. The red light above the camera transfixed her, and Kevin's voice sounded like it came from somewhere far away, as if from down a long corridor. To top things off, she was fighting a chill. The temperature in the blasted television studio had to be set at fifty degrees at the highest. Eva thought about the frigid air a moment and hoped the cold didn't show on her face—or, lord help her—anywhere else on her anatomy. That would be all she needed, for her nipples to make a surprise appearance on national morning television. Eva pushed back a frown as she brought her thoughts back to that blasted red light and Kevin. *Okay, focus time. What is he going on about?*

"I can't marry you," Kevin repeated, and Eva blinked.

Wait. What?

"Wait. What?!" Jim Bauer, *The Morning Show*'s co-host, took Eva's confused thoughts and echoed them out loud, punctuated with his usual everyman laugh. But this was a bad time to laugh. In fact, it was the absolute worst time to laugh. "I don't think we heard you correctly, Kevin. It sounded for a moment like you were calling off the wedding."

Eva fought to keep her smile in place as Kevin turned from her to Jim. "That's right, Jim. I am."

She blinked again as the words really begin to sink in. *He is calling off what?* Anger bubbled up, heating Eva more quickly than could possibly be safe. She caught another glimpse of the red light and forced herself to push it back down. *Hold on there. This is not the time to go off the rails,* Eva told herself. She could do this. She'd practiced being on live TV, and she'd been put on the spot plenty of times. She was trained for these moments. Media relations was her job, for chrissake.

Eva pulled her attention away from the maddening red light that reminded her millions of people were watching this debacle over their morning coffee and toast. Instead, she plastered on a well-trained smile and focused on what her fiancé, Kevin, and the talk show's co-hosts were now saying. But try as she might, she couldn't wrap her head around the words as they trickled toward her in dribs and drabs.

Something about being "confused," Kevin said. "Just not the right time," he went on. And wait, did she really hear the words "moving too fast"?

Hold up, this was madness! It was as if she was having some sort of odd bout of both inner and out-of-body experience, and she couldn't get the two to gel. But she had to, because Kevin was talking about her as if she wasn't there, sitting by his side on TV. National freaking TV! It was time to take control of the situation.

Eva blinked again, her lashes feeling thick and gloppy from the extra coats of mascara plus the individual false lashes the makeup woman had put on her that morning. She had thought they were a bit much at the time. Now she was afraid that with all the ridiculous blinking she was doing, she probably looked like Bambi gone drag. Eva forced her eyes wide, as if that would somehow make her appear saner, and stared at Kevin. Oh hell, Mr. Smooth was starting to sweat, despite the fact that if it was two degrees colder, you'd be able to see your breath as you welcomed Satan into the studio. His sleek, ultra-groomed, dark cocoa skin was starting to glisten, and Eva now noticed a hint of fear in his eyes.

Eva's heart raced, but despite this, she caught Kevin's eye and gave him a smile that she hoped said, "Come on, honey, don't lose your cool now," as she reached over and gave his hand a pat. She could do this. Just a little damage control, and she'd reel this right in.

Eva turned to her other side and looked at Diane Parker, one of *The Morning Show*'s other co-hosts, but Diane's blue eyes only seemed to mirror Eva's own internal confusion.

Just perfect. No help from blondie.

So Eva turned her gaze to Jim. Good ol' Jim. Surely Mr. All America would help save the day. But in that moment, a clear sound finally reached Eva's ears, punctuated by good ol' Jim's good ol' laugh. The loud, false pang rang against her eardrums. "Har, har! Good one, Kevin," Jim said, as Eva took in the obvious tension playing around the corners of his mouth, causing some of his pancake makeup to crease. "Of course you're joking."

"No, Jim, I'm not," Kevin said, his voice clear, strong, and surprisingly absolute as he turned Eva's way. "I'm sorry, Eva. I can't go through with this."

Despite her best efforts at bracing, Eva winced as the words penetrated. The full impact hit her like a crosstown bus trying to make up for lost time.

This was not happening. It couldn't be happening. Not here. Not now. Not to her.

But Kevin continued, his voice getting higher with each word. The more his lips moved and the words washed over her, the more of a blur he became. His handsome features, smooth skin, close-cropped hair, fine button-down oxford shirt, new three-button jacket, pocket square—all becoming a washed-out mass of swirly rejection under the bright studio lights. For a moment, Eva felt like she might be sick, so she bent her head, her gaze hitting Kevin's highly polished leather shoes. The ones that she had picked up for him last week so he would be perfect for their big television appearance this morning. Eva felt her chest tighten as her throat squeezed shut.

"I really am sorry, babe. But I can't do it. It's all too much, and I've realized I'm not ready to get married."

It was like a physical blow. Like he had kicked her in the gut while wearing the shoes she paid for.

Eva's head snapped up then, away from the shoes and away from Kevin too. She saw the camera and the red light as it flashed before her like a beacon. She shut her eyes for a moment and thought once again about how many people watched this while they sipped their morning coffee and ate their sugar-toasted oats. What were they thinking as they stared at the seemingly normal-looking woman in her pink twinset and sharply pleated skirt? Damn it, she was wearing her grandmother's pearls. How does one go about getting dumped in heirloom pearls?

The nausea twisted at her again, and Eva had the distinct feeling that her normally caramel-hued skin was probably taking on a green cast to match the bile now churning in her belly. She wondered if the color would be picked up and broadcast in HD. Now there was ideal breakfast entertainment for you.

And then it hit her, and her worry doubled. Practically tripled. Shit. Her mother was watching this. Watching and most likely fuming. She could imagine the look on Valerie Ward's face right now. She was sure to be yelling into a phone right that moment to have her assistant and the rest of the staff come in early to get started on damage control. The thought sent Eva over the edge. Probably even more than experiencing disappointment herself, she hated the idea of letting her mother down. She'd had enough of that in her life, and though she came off as a human fire-breather, Eva knew it was mostly a mask to cover past hurts.

Not ready to get married.

Kevin's words echoed through Eva's head, along with visions of her mother's impending tirade, and she felt the heat rise. First, it was a burning in the soles of her feet, then it licked up her legs, moving on to radiate through her stomach before finally making its way to her face.

She paused, her breathing virtually stopping a moment as the stomach churning turned to a full-on boil. Was this bastard really breaking up with her on national television merely months, hell, practically weeks, before her perfectly planned wedding?

Eva finally turned and looked at Kevin, fighting hard to keep her emotions in line. She laughed. A belly laugh that would make even ol' Jim proud. *It's a joke. It has to be*. Diane and Jim cautiously joined her in the chuckle and bolstered her spirits. *Whew*. She couldn't believe she'd almost fallen for it. Of course, Kevin would never do that to her. He also had too much riding on this marriage. Too much riding on them. It must have been some silly producer thing. They were always doing something to try and jack up the ratings. And she played along and fell for it, for a moment. She should have known it was a stunt. What better fodder for the gossip mill and ratings than an on-air breakup and makeup from America's, at least for the moment, sweetheart couple? But Kevin knew how important this was. How much this wedding meant to her. To them and their future. Both personally and professionally. But he had been a fool to go for it in the first place and not let her in on the joke.

Eva strained out a smile. "Funny. But come on, sweetie. Joke's over," she said. "Now tell me you were just playing." She turned to the camera and raised a perfectly arched brow. "Tell America you were playing. We will be married and have our dream wedding right here on *The Morning Show* courtesy of Tied Knot Style and Bliss." Eva smiled wide. Her mother would appreciate the advertiser tie-in. One never missed out on the opportunity to thank a sponsor. It was a cardinal rule of marketing. Always keep the sponsors happy and coming back to write another check.

But instead of laughing with her and getting in on the joke, good ol' Jim clammed up and flipped through his blue cards, looking confused, and Diane, well, she was still a grinning zero as she nodded in a bobble-headed way that couldn't quite be declared for or against the joke theory. And wait, was that sweat on her brow now too? *Holy hell.*

Eva looked back at Kevin for reassurance, and he shrugged. *The bastard shrugged!*

"I really am sorry, Eva. You know I always cared for you."

Cared? Did he say *cared?* A rock thudded where her heart was supposed to be. Cared. As in, what you do for your late grandmother, as in how you felt about your childhood dog. Cared, "ed," as in past tense?

Kevin turned to the camera and laid on that old Kevin charm, looking ever so innocent and sincere. "I'm, um, sorry, America. I'd like to apologize to you too. And this is not Eva's fault. It's all me."

Jim piped in, "Well, I'm not really sure what to say here. We'll, well, take a commercial break and be right back?" He then held his ear and with an awkward look turned to Eva. "Oh, uh, I really am sorry; it seems we can't go to commercial. Not for ninety more seconds." Jim gave Eva a look that said, "Tough break, kid."

Eva bit her lip and tried to steady her breathing, since her heart was beating so hard and fast she was sure the mics must be picking up every erratic thump. Crap! In ninety seconds, she was sure to be dead from humiliation.

Diane shifted her eyes away before speaking to the camera. Her voice took on a funereal tone. "We are truly sad to hear of this development. We were all looking forward to your wedding. But I guess now, given the circumstances, and as per the rules of the competition, we'll have to choose another couple." Diane smiled and changed her voice on a dime. "Luckily, we still have Sherri and Brad from Des Moines, who are our runner-up couple. Hey, as they say, it's for the best to find out before the marriage that the two of you don't suit. Don't you think?"

Just perfect. It's now that she turns into a freaking all-star chatterbox, spouting rules and crap.

"No."

The word came out before Eva could stop to think about what she was saying.

"Excuse me?" Diane asked, her wispy brows drawing together. "Maybe you didn't hear what Kevin said. He does not want to marry you."

Eva shot Diane a look that said *Thanks, but no thanks for the clarification,* then turned back to Kevin as he piped up again.

"Yes, Eva." Kevin put his hand across her forearm. "What are you talking about? I said I won't marry you. There won't be a wedding." He rubbed his hand gently across her forearm. Eva looked down at it, not knowing if it was supposed to be comforting or controlling. It didn't matter.

It wasn't either.

She looked up at him, eyes blazing, and jerked her arm away. Then, catching the red light out of the corner of her eye, Eva thought briefly of her mother, before giving Kevin a huge smile that would probably make the most venomous snake proud. "I don't give a damn what you said. I will have my wedding with or without you." It was like a fire had ignited and was rushing through her veins, threatening to burn out of control.

Kevin pulled back, shaking his head. "Eva, come on. Stop, you're not making sense." Then he lowered his voice to a stage whisper, as if the mics still couldn't pick him up. "Plus you're embarrassing yourself.".

For the second time that morning, Eva laughed inappropriately on national TV. *Goody, maybe hysterics are setting in*. She supposed it was natural, given the circumstances.

"Oh, really? Tell me, how can I embarrass myself any more than you already have? Freaking all of America is watching my national dumpation!" She waved her hands wildly in a gesture to the studio. Beyond them there were multiple cameras and overhead lights, and you could see the silhouettes of the burly cameramen nodding their heads in the distance. Behind Eva, Jim, Diane, and Kevin was a large window with people jockeying for their moment of fame, holding up signs saying hi to mom. Eva blew a guy in a cheese hat a kiss when he made an obscene gesture toward his crotch.

She turned back to Kevin and nodded. "See there! I'm already fielding promising offers."

A mumble of laughter traveled throughout the studio. Kevin looked down at the floor. Coward. She should have known he wasn't up to the challenge when she had to push him to retake the bar exam. No, he was ready, after one little setback, to squander it all and spend his life living between her couch and his rich stepfather's bungalow, making it party-hopping off his good looks and charm. Well, no more.

Eva jabbed a finger into his chest, and Kevin looked back up. This time satisfaction nipped at her as she saw a glimmer of anger in his eyes. "Six years! I have wasted six years dealing with your wishy-washy indecisiveness, and here we are about at the finish line, and you go and back out now. Stopping in the fourth quarter? Eighth inning? On the last lap? What kind of man are you? Well, I'll tell you. You're the type to use up all the best years a woman has, and then when it's time to commit, you bail." As she said the words, she felt a lump form in her throat and tears well in her eyes.

Oh hell no. There was no way she would let that happen. No way would she let Kevin know he'd gotten to her.

She swallowed and then continued, "Well, I've got news for you. There are plenty of men who I'm sure would be happy to take your place. Just ask Cheese Head." Eva looked back to the window, but Cheese Head was gone. She guessed the cheese was fine, but apparently pointing out your sausage was a bit much for morning TV. She turned back to Kevin and continued, "No matter, I will still have my wedding. You are replaceable. The question is, Who's got next? I will have my wedding! And I'll have it on the date as planned!" She pointed to the empty spot beside her. "All I have to do is just insert groom here!"

It was then that Eva detected a murmur going through the studio. Oh crap. Did she really say what she had just said out loud? She looked up and saw the red light flashing like a beacon out to New York, Chicago, Iowa, and beyond. And did she really just say it to not only Kevin, but to Jim, Diane, and the rest of America?

Eva closed her eyes. *Oh God. Please make this a bad dream. It has to be.* But when she opened them and focused on everyone around the studio, the same people who had smiled at her with admiration moments ago were all staring at her now like she was the Wicked Witch of the West or someone ready for a straitjacket. *Shit. This dream is way too real.*

Panicked, Eva jumped off the raised stool; pushing back sharply, she heard it crash to the ground behind her as she ran off the set.

"Well, um, that was spirited. We'll be right back, folks, and in our next half hour, bringing romance back into the kitchen!" The irony of Jim's words almost had Eva cringing as they echoed through the studio's speakers. His ridiculous "Har, har, har" laugh kept time with the clanking of Eva's retreating heels.

Thank you so much for purchasing and reading this work by K.M. Jackson. If you enjoyed it please consider leaving a review at your favorite online retailer. It is a wonderful way to help readers find new books.

Also if you would like to read more from me please check out one of my other titles. And if you don't want to miss my new releases,

Follow Kwana on:
Facebook @KMJacksonAuthor
Twitter @KwanaWrites

Go to www.subscribepage.com/j5r4q9 to sign up for K.M.'s Newsletter.

A native New Yorker, Kwana Jackson, who also writes as K.M. Jackson, spent her formative years on the 'A' train where she had two dreams: 1) to be a fashion designer and 2) to be a writer. After spending over ten years designing women's sportswear for various fashion houses this self-proclaimed former fashionista, took the leap of faith and decided to pursue her other dream of being a writer.

Now a *USA Today* Bestseller Kwana has been tapped by *Oprah Magazine, ShondaLand* and NPR for their Best Romance lists.

A mother of now young adult twins, Kwana currently lives in a suburb of New York with her husband. You can find her online at www.kmjackson.com.

www.ingramcontent.com/pod-product-compliance
Lightning Source LLC
LaVergne TN
LVHW041105150826
845673LV00007B/1940